Enid Blyton's
THE CHILDREN
AT GREEN MEADOWS

Would you like to receive the Enid Blyton Newsletter?
It has lots of news about Enid Blyton books, videos, plays, etc.
There are also puzzles and a page for your letters. It is published
three times a year and is free for children who live in the
United Kingdom and Ireland.
If you would like to receive it for a year, please write to:
The Enid Blyton Newsletter, PO Box 357, London WC2E 9HQ
sending your name and address. (UK and Ireland only.)

First published 1949
Reissued 1994 by Dean
an imprint of Reed Consumer Books Limited
Michelin House, 81 Fulham Road, London SW3 6RB
and Auckland, Melbourne, Singapore and Toronto

ISBN 0 603 55326 5

Produced by Mandarin Offset
Printed and bound in China

Enid Blyton's
THE CHILDREN
AT GREEN MEADOWS

DEAN

Contents

1

The Family at Green Meadows

'Mother! Mother! Where are you?' called Francis. 'Do come here a minute. I've found the very first snowdrop out in the garden.'

His mother came out of the back door, drying her hands on a cloth. 'Oh, Francis – did you have to call me just when I was so busy washing up?'

'Yes, I did, Mother,' said the boy. 'You're always busy, anyway, so it wouldn't matter when I called you. I wish you weren't so busy. Fancy not even having time to look at a snowdrop! See, there it is!'

His mother looked down and saw the tiny white flower with its pretty drooping head. It grew in a mass of tangled grass, in a corner of the garden. She bent down and shook it gently.

'I know why you do that!' said Francis. 'I *knew* you would. It's lucky to ring the bell of the first snowdrop you see in the new year, isn't it?'

His mother laughed. 'That's what country folk say, Francis – and goodness knows we could do with a little good luck!'

She looked round the big, rambling garden and slipped her arm through the boy's. 'I'm not too busy to walk round to see if anything else is coming up,' she said. 'It's St Valentine's Day, the day all the birds marry – listen to them singing! Even the starling up on the chimney is doing his best – he never has learnt that he can't sing properly!'

Francis was glad to have his mother for a few minutes. He remembered a time when she was always ready to run into the garden, to play, to plant seeds, to weed – when she laughed a lot and looked young and happy. Now things were very different, and it was quite a treat to have his mother to himself for a few minutes.

'There's a crocus peeping up,' she said. 'And look, over there is actually a violet – in that sheltered corner at the foot of the wall. Let's see if there are any primroses in the dell at the bottom of the garden.'

There weren't. It was too early. His mother stood in the dell under the silver birch trees, and fell silent. Francis looked at her. He touched her gently.

'What are you thinking about? Why do you look like that?'

'I was just remembering how this garden looked four years ago,' said his mother. 'It was beautiful, Francis! You were almost eight then – you must remember it too.'

'Yes. The grass was cut, the beds were weeded, there were thousands of flowers,' said the boy, looking back through the years. 'The house was different too, Mother. We didn't have half the rooms shut up like we do now – and you weren't so busy – and . . .'

He stopped because he saw tears in his mother's eyes. 'Why are we so poor now?' he asked. 'Why don't we get a gardener to put the garden right? Why do you do all the work in the big house? Is it because of Daddy?'

'Partly,' said his mother. 'Daddy was badly hurt in the war, you know, and he can't work any more, so we haven't much to live on. Granny let us have this house when we were first married, Daddy and I – it's hers, you know – and I was glad, because I was brought up here as a little girl. I knew every corner.'

'Well – why can't we let Granny have it back, and go and live in a smaller place?' said Francis. Then, looking round the old garden he knew so well, he suddenly changed his mind. 'No. No, I didn't mean that. I couldn't bear to leave Green Meadows! It's our home – Granny's home, yours, and mine.'

'I feel the same,' said his mother, 'but things are getting so difficult that I feel we shall *have* to leave soon, Francis – if only we could sell the house! But it is in such a bad state now that nobody wants it – it's too big a house nowadays, you see. And anyway, Granny won't hear of selling it – so I really don't know what we are to do.'

She went to the old wall that ran all round the garden, and looked over it. Not far off an enormous building was going up – a great block of flats. Another one, almost finished, was just behind it.

'Not many years ago this was all countryside,' she told Francis. 'That's why this house was called Green Meadows – when it was first built we could see nothing but green fields all round, stretching right to those hills over there. Now all the fields are going to be a housing estate – look at those blocks of flats!'

'Well – it will mean that more children come to the village,' said Francis. 'That will be more fun for us. But I suppose we'll be a town then. We've already got more shops, and a brand-new post office.'

His mother turned to go in, suddenly remembering the washing-up she had to do. She gave Francis a pat on the arm. 'Don't you worry about it, now. These are grown-up worries, not yours. I don't know why I told you so much. I'm all muddled somehow. I want to go on living here in Green Meadows, which I love so much – but not in this mess and muddle, not when I have to do so much that I've hardly time for you and the other two children. And . . .'

Francis finished for her. 'And anyway Granny won't sell the house, so we've got to make the best of it! I wish I could make the garden nice for you, Mother – but it's so big! I'm a Scout, you know, and I'm willing to help any way I can. And Clare is a Brownie, and Sam's a Cub – you can *always* ask us to do anything!'

'I do!' said his mother. 'But I'm not going to put old heads on young shoulders. Go and ask Daddy if he wants anything, Francis. There! I've asked you to do something already!'

She went slowly indoors. Francis watched her. She looked sad and her merry smile hardly ever came now. 'I wish I was grown up!' thought Francis. 'It takes so *long* to grow up! I can't earn a penny – all I can do is to run errands and clean the shoes and things like that. Any Scout can do that. I want to do something that will really help!'

But he knew he couldn't. Grown-ups had to manage their own affairs. He went to find his father. It wasn't difficult because he lived all day long in a wheelchair and was never far away.

'Do you want anything, Dad?' asked Francis. 'How's your back?'

'Same as usual,' said his father. 'Can't you go and help your mother a bit, Francis? I hate to sit here and see her tearing about hard at work all day long – I feel so useless. Go and help her.'

'She sent me to ask you if *you* wanted anything,' said Francis, with a good-tempered grin. 'When's the doctor coming again, Dad? Isn't the new treatment any good?'

'Not a bit. Nothing ever will be, I'm sure,' said his father. 'If only you were older, Francis! Your mother's got too much on her shoulders.'

'I've just been thinking exactly the same thing,' said Francis. 'Mother's been talking to me and telling me a lot this morning. I don't want to leave Green Meadows, Dad, but for Mother's sake I think we should. She'll kill herself! She has so much to do. Won't Granny sell the house, won't she really?'

'No, she won't,' said Daddy, shortly. 'Now that she has come back to live with us here she seems to love the old place more than ever, tumbledown though it is. Let's not talk about it, or I shall get angry.'

Francis heard his mother calling and went off. What a tangle! He couldn't see what in the world was to be done! Granny was a difficult person to get on with – very touchy and thinking far too much about herself. All three of her grandchildren were afraid of her sharp tongue – and yet at times she could be so unexpectedly kind.

There was the sound of running feet on the path outside. The back door burst open and in came Clare and Sam. Clare was nine, big for her age, curly-haired and bright-eyed. Sam was seven, small and solemn, and seldom laughed – but when he did it was always a surprise, because his laugh was loud and very sudden. It made everyone else laugh too.

'We're back, Mother!' called Clare. 'We had a jolly good meeting at the Brownies.'

'So did we at the Cubs,' said Sam. 'I'm the smallest there, but I'm not the worst. I'd better not tell you who is the worst.'

'He's *bursting* to tell us,' said Clare. 'Don't be a tell-tale, Sam. Anyway, we know the answer. Mother, can I have something to eat? I don't think I can wait till dinnertime. It's ages since breakfast!'

An old lady came into the kitchen. She jingled as she came, for she wore several chains about her – a long gold one that reached to her waist and was fastened to a gold watch tucked into her belt – a silvery one with a locket on it, round her neck – and a chain bracelet on each of her wrists, fastened by tiny padlocks.

'I always know when you are coming, Granny!' said Clare. 'You jingle like the coal man's horse!'

'I don't think that's very polite,' said Granny. 'I'm not in the least like the coal man's horse.'

'Clare thinks the coal man's jingling horse is lovely,' explained Sam at once. 'So do I. I'd like to jingle when I walk about, too. I think . . .'

'That's enough,' said Granny. She turned to her daughter, the children's mother. 'No wonder you haven't finished yet!' she said. 'I saw you wandering about in the garden with Francis, talking away like anything! Why don't you finish everything first – then you might have time for a rest in the afternoon.'

Granny took up a duster and a tin of polish and began rubbing the furniture hard. That was exactly like Granny – to scold and then to do what she could to help. The three children ran out of the room. They felt sure that Granny would think of something unpleasant to say if they stayed there!

Francis opened a door on the landing upstairs. The room inside was quite empty, but it had a window seat under the big bow window. 'Come on,' said Francis. 'Let's sit down and eat our biscuits here, and pretend it's our old playroom again!'

It had once been their playroom, but, like so many of the other rooms, its furniture had been sold and the room left empty and unused. The children often crept in there and sat on the window seat.

'It's got such a nice feel about it, this room,' said Clare, nibbling her biscuit. 'It's a happy room, even though it's got nothing to be happy about now. I expect it keeps remembering all the old dolls and teddy bears and trains that Granny and her brothers played with . . .'

'And that Mummy and *her* brothers and sisters had . . .'

'And the ones we had, too, when we still had this room

for our own,' said Francis. 'You don't remember that very well, Sam. You were too little.'

Clare looked out of the window. 'Look at that enormous block of flats,' she said. 'The one that's finished. Someone must have moved into one of the flats, because I can see two children. It seems funny to see those great buildings instead of green fields. Oh, well – I don't expect they'll make much difference to *us*!'

Ah, you wait and see, Clare! You'll be surprised!

There was always plenty for the three children to do at Green Meadows. Out of school hours there were endless jobs to be done. Even Sam helped.

Their mother never nagged them to do their jobs, however tired she was. But Granny did! She was always after them, asking if this had been done and that had been done – and who was supposed to get the wood in for the fire, and why had it been left to the last moment?

Francis and Sam were patient, but Clare was hot-tempered. Often she came storming to find her mother.

'Mother! Granny says I don't think about you enough! I *do* think about you, and Granny's not to say that!'

'Oh darling – you haven't been rude to Granny, have you?' her mother would say. 'Her tongue may be sharp but her heart is kind. It's only because she's worried about me that she says these things. *I* know you think of me – that's all that matters, isn't it? That *I* shall know?'

'Yes, I suppose it is,' Clare would say, and smile and give her mother a hug. And then the very next day Granny's tongue would upset her again, and there would be another storm.

'I don't believe Granny loves any of us,' Sam said solemnly one evening. 'She scolds us all, Daddy and Mother too – but there's only one person she doesn't scold, so she must love him very much.'

'Who's that?' said Clare, surprised. 'You don't mean Dr Miles, do you? She's fond of him because she thinks he tries to help Daddy.'

'No. I mean Mr Black,' said Sam. Everyone roared with laughter. Mr Black was Granny's cat, an enormous fellow with great yellow eyes, a wonderful tail, and fur like thick shiny silk. He was as black as soot. He had been called Blackie when he was a kitten – but he grew up so big and solemn and high-and-mighty that Granny felt she couldn't call him by such an ordinary name as Blackie.

So she called him Majesty because he looked so majestic. He didn't answer to that name at all, of course, because he didn't know it. So then the family called him Mr Black, and that was all right. It sounded enough like 'Blackie' to him, and he came when he was called.

He belonged to Granny, and she loved him with all her heart. Blackie adored her too, and always slept in a basket in Granny's room.

He was a very spoilt cat. The three children made a great fuss of him, for they were all fond of animals. Sometimes they talked about Thumper, a beautiful Great Dane who had belonged to Granny some years back. His great paws thumped about the house all day long. As Clare said, you always knew where Thumper was, you couldn't help it, he stamped about so!

'He was so lovely,' said Clare, remembering. 'He was as big as I was, but he was as gentle as a kitten.'

'Kittens aren't always gentle,' said Sam, who liked every statement to be quite correct. 'When Mr Black was a kitten he bit me.'

'Do you remember when Thumper wagged his big tail to greet a visitor one afternoon, and swept all the cakes off the cake-stand on the little table?' said Francis.

Sam thought that was very funny. He gave one of his sudden roars of laughter. 'I wish I'd seen that,' he said. 'What happened to Thumper? I don't remember. And why aren't we allowed to talk about him to Granny?'

'Well, it cost an awful lot to feed a big dog like that,' said Francis. 'So one day Granny decided it wasn't fair on the family to keep him any longer.'

'Oh,' said Sam, looking solemn again. 'What did she do with him then?'

'She sold him,' said Francis. 'He was a very valuable dog, and she got a lot of money for him. After that she didn't have to feed him, of course, so she saved a lot of money too. Granny loved Thumper. More than she loves Mr Black.'

'Did she cry?' asked Sam, looking very serious.

'She cried for two whole days,' said Francis. 'She couldn't stop. She said we weren't to take any notice of her, she would get over it. You don't remember that, Sam.'

'Granny's fond of animals,' said Clare. 'She's told us all about those she had when she was a child. She was lucky. All we've got is Mr Black, and he doesn't *really* belong to us.'

'No, he's Granny's,' said Sam. 'I wish we had animals of our own. I'd like a rabbit. And some mice. And plenty of hens. I'd like a monkey too, and perhaps a small bear.'

'I'd like dogs,' said Francis. 'Plenty of them! And puppies and kittens.'

'I'd like birds,' said Clare. 'Pigeons that fly about the garden. There's an old pigeon-house here still lying broken down in one corner, isn't there? I expect Granny kept pigeons there once. She had a horse too, called Clover.'

'If we were well-off we could have heaps and heaps of animals,' said Sam. 'I like them better than toys. They are alive and they can love you. I love toys – but I'm never *really* certain they ever love me back!'

'Sometimes,' said Clare, suddenly, looking at Francis out of the corner of her eyes, '*sometimes* I think you must have a dog of your own, Francis!'

'Well, I haven't,' said Francis, shortly. To Sam's enormous surprise he went bright red, and turned his face away.

'You've gone red,' said Sam. 'You're hiding something from us! You always go red when you do that. So do I.'

'Let's go out and do something,' said Francis, getting up. 'I've finished my biscuit.'

He went out of the room. They heard him going down the stairs. Sam looked solemnly at Clare. 'What did you mean when you said you sometimes thought that Francis had a dog of his own, Clare? He hasn't, has he?'

'No. Not really,' said Clare. 'But it's funny, Sam – when Francis thinks he's alone and nobody's watching

him, he holds out his hands, and says, "Come on, Paddy
– walkie – walk!" Just like that – as if a dog was behind
him.'

Sam thought about this. 'He's pretending a dog,' he
said. 'I know he wants one badly. So do I. When do you
see Francis doing this?'

'Oh, often,' said Clare. 'Sometimes I'm in the garden,
behind the hedge – and Francis comes along by himself
and talks to his dog then. The other day he threw a ball
for him, and said, "Bring it back, Paddy – that's right!
Good dog!" And he bent and patted the air!'

'I'm not going to say anything about this dog to him,'
said Sam. 'If he'd wanted to share him with us he would
have told us about him. Does the dog go to bed with him,
and sleep on his feet, I wonder?'

'I don't know,' said Clare. 'You sleep in the same
room. You can watch and see.'

'I'm always asleep when Francis comes to bed,' said
Sam. 'Always. Even if I try to keep awake I can't. And
anyway I'm not going to pry into Francis's secret. And
don't you either, Clare! See?'

'You stop telling me what I'm to do or not to do!' said
Clare. 'A little shrimp like you! I wish I hadn't told you
about the pretend dog now. I shan't say anything about it
to Francis – unless he teases me about something, and
then I'll tease him back – about Paddy!'

'That would be mean of you!' called Sam, as Clare
walked out of the room. She slammed the door. Sam
didn't mind. He was used to Clare's sudden bursts of

temper. She would have forgotten it the next time he saw her, and be as friendly as ever.

He thought about Francis's pretend dog. Poor old Francis! How he must want a dog of his own to invent one like that! He was like Granny – he really loved animals. He patted every dog he saw and spoke to it. He fed the wild birds in the garden. Every cat came to him as soon as it saw him. The milkman's horse walked right across the road, cart and all, if he heard Francis's voice!

'And when he went to the Zoo and Francis spoke to the monkeys in the cage, they left everything they were doing and came crowding to the wire,' Sam remembered. 'They put their tiny paws through the wire and tried to take his fingers – though he hadn't any food to give them! They chattered like anything too – I was sure they were telling him they wanted to be friends.'

The door opened and Granny looked in. 'Sam! What are you doing here all alone?'

'Just thinking,' said Sam

'You think too much,' said Granny. 'You're too serious altogether! It's not good for you to sit up here, mooning away by yourself.'

'I wasn't mooning,' said Sam, getting up. 'What *is* mooning, Granny? Is it anything to do with the moon?'

'Oh, don't be *silly*, Sam!' said Granny. 'Do go on down and give a hand somewhere.'

'Well, here's a hand!' said Sam, and suddenly slipped his into Granny's. 'Shall I do something for *you*? Then you won't feel so cross.'

Granny looked down at the hand in hers, and gave a sudden laugh. She squeezed Sam's hand. 'You're a caution!' she said. 'No, please don't ask me what a caution is! It's something quite nice when I call *you* one. Let's go and dig some potatoes, shall we? The potato basket is getting empty.'

'I'll dig them. Don't bother,' said Sam. 'I'll get the spade and the trug now.'

He went off to the old stables that belonged to Green Meadows. The horse-stalls were still there, and the harness room led off one end, a place where the family put all their junk. It was always exciting to Sam to look through the junk and rubbish piled in the corners and on the shelves.

He stood in the stables and looked round, pretending that he could hear the stamp-stamp, clop-clop of horses' hooves. Did Francis pretend a horse too that lived in the stables? Over the mangers were little brass plates, green with age, still bearing the names of long-ago horses.

'Dapple'. That was a pretty name for a horse, Sam thought.

'Clopper'. 'Benjy'. 'Captain'. They all sounded nice. He must ask Granny about them. Perhaps they were horses she knew back in history, when she was a little girl.

'Sam! I thought you were going to dig potatoes!' Oh dear – that was Granny's voice! Sam picked up the trug and the spade and began to dig vigorously. He liked it. The birds sang all round him, and the sun was warm on the back of his neck. He pursed up his lips and tried to whistle, a thing he had never been able to do, much to his shame.

A loud whistle came suddenly from his lips, startling Sam very much. He pursed up his mouth and tried again. Another whistle, as loud as the blackbirds near by, came at once. Sam went red with delight. He could whistle at last!

'It's my lucky day!' thought Sam. 'I can suddenly whistle. Now I shan't be the only Cub that can't!'

And whistling loudly and tunelessly, Sam dug up half a row of potatoes. Who would ever have thought that whistling was such a help to hard work?

2

Two Unexpected Fights!

February slipped into March, and the winds came, the mad March winds that shook the trees in the gardens of Green Meadows and 'blew the birds about the sky'.

The days had gone by very quietly, and nothing much had happened except that Mr Black had most unexpectedly mixed himself up in a fight with two other cats. This had caused great excitement at Green Meadows.

It had happened at night. Everyone but Sam had been suddenly awakened by a screaming, yowling, squealing noise just under the windows. Everyone had sat up straight in bed, their hearts beating fast. Oh, whatever could it be?

It was two strange cats fighting down in the garden. It sounded exactly as if they were killing one another. Daddy groaned. 'If only I could get out of bed and walk to the window I'd empty a jug of water over them!' he said. 'Making a row like this in the middle of the night. If it's Mr Black I'll tell him what I think of him in the morning!'

But it wasn't Mr Black. Granny's big black cat had been asleep as usual in his basket in Granny's own room.

The yowling had wakened him at once and he sat up, looking huge, his tail swelling out till it was twice its usual size.

Mr Black was furious. What were strange cats doing in his garden? How *dare* they? He leapt from his basket, jumped on to the windowsill, through the open window to a pear tree below – and then leapt straight down on top of the two fighting cats. He must have seemed like a cannonball to them!

Granny was soon at her window, calling in anguish. 'Mr Black! Mr Black! Stop it, now! Oh, he'll get killed! Oh, I must stop this fight!'

And there was Granny rushing down the stairs in her dressing gown, ready to tear her beloved Mr Black away from two clawing cats!

But before she or Francis could get there – Francis was close behind her – the cats had moved on over the wall, pursued by an extremely angry Mr Black, who spat and hissed and used his enormous claws wherever he could. The noise faded into the distance, and Granny sat down suddenly on the seat in the porch.

'Oh dear – what a shock I got! Oh, Francis, where are they? What has happened to Mr Black? He'll be torn to pieces!'

'It's all right, Granny. He'll come back, all puffed up with pride, to tell you how he sent away two cat burglars!' said Francis, trying to make his grandmother laugh. She couldn't help giving a little smile. 'Help me up the stairs, Francis,' she said. 'A sudden scare like that makes me feel an old woman!'

Mr Black didn't come back that night, so the next morning Granny was tired out. 'I haven't been to sleep all night,' she said. 'Where can Mr Black be?'

Clare nudged Sam. 'Don't you start your whistling again now,' she warned him. 'Granny will be ever so cross today!'

Sam nudged Clare back, but much harder. 'Don't keep on so about my whistling,' he said. 'It's a very *new* whistle, and I've got to practise it. Granny – I'll go and look for Mr Black for you, shall I?'

But Mr Black came back after dinner, much to everyone's joy. Granny certainly *had* been cross and Mother was certain that Clare was going to fly into a fury very soon, because Granny nagged her so much!

Mr Black came sauntering across the grass just after the family had finished their dinner. Daddy saw him first. 'Here's our Mr Black,' he announced from his wheelchair. 'Large as life and looking very pleased with himself. The warrior returned home from the wars!'

Granny gave a little squeal and rose from her chair at once. She ran to the window and flung it open.

'Mr Black! Are you all right?'

Mr Black didn't even look at her. He sat down in the middle of the grass, cocked up one of his legs and began to wash himself very thoroughly indeed.

'He's showing off!' said Clare. 'I'll fetch him in for you, Granny.'

But, exactly as if he had heard what Clare had said, Mr Black stood up and ran to the window. In two seconds he was in Granny's arms, and she was exclaiming over him.

'Mr Black! You've got a bitten ear! And oh dear, look, children – he's got a bare patch on his tail. Oh, *why* did you mix yourself up in a fight, Mr Black? Where's some ointment, children?'

Daddy began to growl, as he always did when Granny made too much fuss over Mr Black. 'Fussing over him like that – as if he were a baby! Honestly, it makes me feel sick the way you treat that cat! He can expect a bitten ear and tail if he fights. *He* doesn't mind them, so why should you?'

Granny flashed round at him at once. 'You don't love animals. I don't believe you even *like* them!'

'I do,' said Daddy. 'But I don't believe in gushing over them, that's all. You know I loved Thumper.'

There was a silence. Thumper, Granny's long-ago Great Dane, was not supposed to be mentioned by anyone. Granny looked at Daddy.

'Yes,' she said. 'I know you did. All the same, I still say you don't really l . . .'

'Yes, Daddy does, yes, Daddy does,' began Clare, who always rushed to her father's help if Granny attacked him. Granny attacked everyone at times. 'Yes, Daddy does, yes, Daddy does, yes . . .'

'Clare!' said Mummy. 'Fetch the ointment, please – at once!'

Mr Black loved all the fuss and bother. He purred as loudly as a sewing machine!

'He's a fraud,' said Daddy under his breath to Clare. She nodded. 'Yes – but he's a *nice* fraud!' she answered.

Mr Black's adventure was the biggest thing that

happened in those few quiet weeks when the crocuses gave place to the early daffodils, and primroses began to come out in the dell. Francis went on with his pretending, and his pretend-dog, Paddy, went with him everywhere. Clare tried to learn knitting from Granny, who thought it was time she was taught – but Granny was too impatient a teacher and Clare was too hot-tempered a pupil, so it didn't come to anything.

Sam's great thrill was his new whistle, which he practised so continually that he nearly drove everyone mad. Sam was upset to think his family didn't share his delight in this great new gift of his, and at last he took to going to the stables, and shutting himself in. There he whistled to his heart's content – trying his hardest to whistle a tune, but never quite succeeding!

And then something quite unusual happened. It happened to Francis one evening when he was going home from a Scouts' meeting. As usual he had his pretend dog, Paddy, with him. There was no one in the lane he was walking down, so he gave his dog practice in coming to him when he whistled.

He had his Scout whistle with him, and he blew it. Then he signalled with his hand to Paddy, who was supposed to be a hundred or so yards away.

Paddy galloped up at once when the whistle sounded. 'Good, Paddy!' said Francis. 'Very good! Try again. This time, stop when I put up my hand like this!'

The dog was so real to him that Francis actually thought he could see the dog's tail wagging, and his pink tongue hanging out of his mouth. He could hear the dog panting! Pretends can be very, very real.

'Run off to the same place, Paddy,' said Francis. 'When I whistle, come running – but stop when I put up my hand. Stop dead! Now!'

He whistled – and then two seconds later put up his hand. 'Good!' called Francis. 'Good dog! Now come to heel and walk with your nose just touching my ankle.'

He could almost feel the dog's nose touching his ankle as he began to walk down the lane again. And then he heard something that made him jump. It was a loud jeering laugh.

'Ha ha! You're crazy, aren't you? Talking to a dog that isn't there!'

Francis looked all round but could see nobody. Then he heard a noise nearby, and a boy slid down a tree, leaping to the ground from the lowest branch.

He was a bit taller than Francis, about thirteen, dirty and untidy. His hair stood up in a shock, dark brown and curly, and his mouth was curved in a jeering grin.

Francis didn't know what to say. He couldn't possibly explain to anyone about Paddy, the dog he had made up – especially not to a jeering boy like this. So he just said nothing and walked on.

The boy put his fingers to his mouth and gave such a shrill, piercing whistle that Francis jumped. 'Paddy, Paddy!' called the boy, trying to imitate Francis's voice. 'Good dog, then. Walk to heel! That's right – nose to my ankle!'

Francis was speechless. The boy actually bent down and pretended to pat a dog! Then he began to walk towards Francis, looking down as if the dog were at his heels. 'Good!' he said. 'Fine!'

'Shut up,' said Francis, temper welling up in him suddenly and powerfully.

'Yah!' said the boy. 'He's *my* dog now! He won't follow *you* any more! I'm going to take him home to lie with my own dog. He wants companionship!'

'I said shut up,' said Francis, and he felt his fists clenching themselves tightly.

'You're a Scout. Scouts mustn't fight. Naughty, naughty!' said the aggravating boy. 'Why don't you get a *real* dog, instead of a silly pretend one? You're potty!'

Francis said nothing. He was so angry now that he couldn't even speak.

'I've got a beauty!' said the boy. 'You should see him, he's a – well, he's a sort of spaniel: but he's real, not like your silly Paddy-dog! Here, Paddy, Paddy, let me put a lead on you and take you home to Rex. Come on, boy!'

And the boy bent down and pretended to tie a bit of string to a dog's collar. Francis never really knew what happened then – he just felt his fist hitting the boy's downbent face – biff!

And then something struck Francis on the side of the head – the big boy's clenched fist. The fight was on! Biff! Thud! Biff!

It could only end one way. The other boy was taller and stronger – and in half a minute's time Francis found himself lying flat on the ground, seeing stars all round him! The other boy went off, laughing loudly.

And to make things worse, he was calling Paddy.

'Paddy. Come along then! Don't you even bother to lick his wounds! He's not worth it. You come along with me!'

Francis sat up, feeling dazed. The lane seemed to go round and round him, hedges and all. He shut his eyes, feeling suddenly ashamed of himself.

He was a Scout – and yet he had provoked a fight with another boy. He hadn't even the excuse that he had had to defend himself. But – how could he have helped it? The boy had jeered and sneered at his secret – and had actually said he had got Paddy on a lead and was going to take him home!

Francis stood up and went to lean over a nearby gate. He felt in a muddle. He tried to sort it out, but he couldn't. He felt that he had done right, it was the only thing he could do – yet he knew it was wrong too.

He went home, hoping that he didn't look too dreadful. His left eye felt very tender, and his right cheek felt strange. He could see quite a lot of it with his right eyes, and usually he couldn't see his cheeks at all!

He slipped in at the garden door, hoping that he could get up to his bedroom unseen. His granny heard him and called him.

'Is that you, Francis? Come in here a minute, will you?'

'I'll just go upstairs first and wash, Granny,' called Francis, and rushed up the stairs before his grandmother could see him. He went into his room and looked into the mirror on the wall.

What a sight he looked! What a dreadful sight! His left eye was almost shut now, and a purple bruise was coming up round it. His right cheek was red and swollen. He hurriedly went to the bathroom and began to wash his face in cold water.

His heart suddenly sank – Granny had come upstairs after him, cross because he hadn't come when she called him. 'Francis! Why didn't you . . .' she began, and then stopped. 'What are you washing your face for? Are you hurt?'

'I'm all right, Granny, thank you,' said Francis, desperately. 'I'm just coming.'

Granny lifted his head and made him look at her. 'You're hurt! You've had an accident! What's happened?'

'Nothing. I tell you it's nothing,' said Francis. 'Just a little swelling.'

'You've been fighting!' said Granny, in horror. 'Don't deny it! You a Scout too! Oh, to think of it!'

She went downstairs. Francis felt miserable. He held his nose and put his whole head into the basin of water, hoping that that would help his eye and cheek. He felt a tap on his shoulder and took his head out of the water.

It was Clare. 'Francis! What's happened? Granny's telling everyone you've been fighting. Are you hurt?'

'No!' said Francis, fiercely. 'All this fuss! Anyone would think there had never been a fight before!'

'But *you*, Francis – you're so peaceful,' said Clare. 'Francis – do tell me what it was all about? I do want to know. It's the first fight our family has ever been in.'

Francis dried his face very gingerly indeed, and brushed and combed his hair.

'You look awful,' said Clare. 'Don't you feel important, Francis, looking like that because of a fight?'

'Why are girls so silly?' exploded Francis, who was longing to be alone so that he could think out all that had happened so very suddenly. He pushed Clare aside and went to his room. Clare followed.

'Mother says you are to come straight down,' said Clare. 'And don't you push me about like that.'

'If you don't go away at once I'll *shove* you,' said poor Francis. Clare disappeared. Francis glared at himself in the glass, what a sight! Well, it wasn't any good staying up in his room – the whole family would be trailing up the stairs to find him! He might as well go down and face the music.

So down he went. As soon as he opened the door of the sitting room everyone looked up. There were sudden gasps and exclamations.

'Francis, dear! Your poor face!'

'What did I tell you? He's been fighting!'

'He wouldn't tell me a thing!' said Clare.

Sam just stared solemnly after his first gasp. How peculiar Francis looked – not like Francis at all.

'How did it happen, dear?' asked his mother, gently. She pulled him to her. Thank goodness – she wasn't going to be too cross! Francis was relieved. What about his father? Would he be angry, like Granny?

It was Granny who scolded him loudly and angrily. Nobody else said a word. At last his father interrupted.

'That's enough,' he said. 'Leave the boy alone. He's not one to fight without a reason – and most boys get into fights sooner or later. Even Scouts have to fight to defend themselves! Did someone attack you, Francis?'

Francis longed to say, 'Yes – and I had to defend myself.' But it was wrong and cowardly to lie like that, and he wasn't going to begin. He shook his head.

'What happened then?' said his father, in astonishment. 'Speak up, Francis. We only want to know.'

'I – well – I just hit someone, that's all,' said Francis. 'He, er – he said and – and did something I didn't like – and I hit him.'

There was silence. 'So *you* began the fight?' said his father. 'I see. What did the boy say and do that you didn't like? Surely you can tell us that?'

'No, I can't,' said Francis, shutting up in his most secret heart his pretence about Paddy the dog. He felt rather peculiar, for he could only see out of one eye now. The left one had gradually swelled up and was shut.

Granny began again. 'I do think, I really do think that . . .'

'There is to be no more said unless I say it!' said Daddy, in such a determined voice that everyone was startled. Granny stood up, offended.

'Very well, then – if I can't say what I want to *in my own house*, I'll leave you to it!' And she marched out, stiff and straight as a walking stick.

Mother sighed. 'Oh dear! Francis, let me put something on that eye.'

'Who won the fight?' asked Sam, suddenly.

'I didn't,' said Francis.

'I bet the boy was bigger and older than you,' said Sam. 'Else you'd have beaten him. Knocked him down flat. Biff-thud!'

'Be quiet, Sam,' said his mother. 'Come with me, Francis.'

Mother was kind. She put something comforting on his eye, and patted his shoulder, and didn't ask him a single question. Francis squeezed her arm.

'I'd tell you if I could, Mother, but I can't,' he said. 'Not yet, anyhow.'

'That's all right, dear. Everybody has some secret or other – and why not?' said his mother. 'You shouldn't start a fight, you know that; but if you did I'm quite prepared to believe that you just had to. So don't worry about it.'

But Francis did worry, of course. Suppose the Scoutmaster got to hear of it? Suppose that boy spread the news around about the dog he had invented, and everyone laughed at him? Suppose, suppose, suppose!

At last he had to tell someone. He told Clare. After all, she already knew about his pretend dog, and she wouldn't laugh if he told her it was something serious – surely she wouldn't?

'Clare – come up into the old playroom,' Francis said, two days after the fight. His face looked very peculiar, and he had had a lot of teasing from the boys in his class, but his cheek was not so swollen now, and he could eat without difficulty. Clare nodded.

'All right. I'll just finish laying the table, and I'll come.'

She came to join him on the window seat in the playroom. Francis began at once. 'It's about the fight. I'm awfully worried, Clare, and I've simply got to tell someone. But don't laugh, will you?'

Clare shook her head vigorously. 'No, of course not. Tell me.'

So Francis told her the whole thing – how the boy up the tree had seen him teaching Paddy, the invented dog, to be obedient, and how he had jeered and laughed; and at last how he had pretended to put Paddy on a lead and take him home with him.

'Oh! What a horrible boy,' said Clare. 'And you say he'd got a dog of his own too? Fancy wanting to take yours! No wonder you hit him. I would have, too.'

'It all happened so suddenly,' said Francis. 'What worries me is that I hit him first – and you see, if I tell Daddy or Mother or Granny the whole truth, they would think I was *crazy* to start a fight about a pretend dog. Anyway, I can't tell anyone about Paddy! Except you – and you knew.'

'Don't worry about it,' said Clare, comfortingly. 'What's it matter now? You've still got Paddy, and if I were you I'd teach him to go and *bite* that boy if ever you see him again.'

'I can't,' said Francis. 'I haven't got him any more.'

'Where is he then?' cried Clare, astonished.

'Well, you know what pretends are – they sometimes go, all of a sudden,' said Francis. 'Like when we pretended there was a bear in the old stables and wouldn't go near them. And suddenly the pretend stopped and we knew there wasn't a bear there.'

'Yes. But that was because we wanted to go and hunt through that old junk in the harness room,' said Clare. 'Still – you're right. Pretends do go all of a sudden. Has Paddy really gone? Perhaps that boy is pretending him instead of you? Why don't you get another dog?'

Francis stared at her. 'I tried that,' he said. 'But one won't come. I mean – it's just pretend and nothing else. Paddy seemed real. Oh Clare, I do wish I had a pet of my own. A horse. Or a dog. Or even pigeons.'

'Perhaps if you did *two* good deeds a day instead of one, you'd get what you want,' said Clare. 'Anyway, I'll put a dog in my prayers each night for you. Do cheer up, Francis. It's awful to see you going about so gloomy. You make Mother worried.'

'Well, I do feel better since I've told you,' said Francis, looking more cheerful. 'Don't tell anyone, will you?'

'As if I should,' said Clare, scornfully. 'I'm a Brownie, aren't I? Well then, you ought to trust me. Anyway, you know I always keep my word.'

She ran downstairs, proud that Francis had told her his worry and no one else. That horrid boy! 'I'd like to smack him hard!' thought Clare, fiercely. 'And if I ever meet him, I will! But I don't expect I ever shall!'

She did though – the very next day!

3

That Boy Again!

Francis was late home from school the next day because it was his week to keep the shelves tidy.

'I'm always glad when it's a Scout's turn to be the monitor for the week,' said his teacher. 'I don't even need to see if the job is done properly. I only wish the whole class were Scouts!'

Francis was pleased. He spent an extra long time doing the job perfectly. Then he went home, half an hour late.

Clare and Sam were watching for him, over the wall. They wanted to tell him that Granny had been in a very good mood all day long, and had bought some special chocolate biscuits for tea.

'Here he comes,' said Clare to Sam. 'Don't say a word till he gets to the gate. Then we'll yell out "Chocolate biscuits", and make him jump.'

But before they could yell, somebody else yelled first. 'Hey! Come here, Paddy! He's not your master any more! Come here, boy! That's right, that's right!'

Francis swung round. The boy he had fought stood just across the road, laughing. He bent down and pretended to pat a dog. He crossed the road, looking down as if the dog was at his heels, and stood just under the wall near Clare and Sam. He didn't see them, he was watching Francis.

'Did you miss your dog?' he yelled. Francis swung in through the gate, slammed it, and went up the path, fuming. Horrible, horrible boy!

The boy laughed jeeringly – and then he suddenly stopped. Someone fell on him, someone pummelled him hard, someone pulled his hair and panted out, 'Take that – and that – and that! Oh, you nasty horrid thing!'

The boy shook off the someone and raised his fist to strike. Then he dropped it suddenly.

'Gosh!' he said. 'It's a girl! What do you think you're doing, you fathead?'

'This,' said Clare, and hit out at him fiercely. The boy dodged, the blow missed, and Clare fell over on the ground with a bump.

'I don't fight little girls!' said the boy. 'Or little boys either!' he added, as Sam suddenly landed beside him. 'What's up, you two? Why are you behaving like this?'

'You give Paddy back,' said Clare, standing up and scowling. 'My brother loves dogs and he'd give anything to have one of his own. You've got one. You're very, very lucky. You be careful *your* dog doesn't come to my brother now you've taken his!'

'Don't be silly,' said the boy. 'Paddy's only a silly pretend. As for my dog, he'd never, never go to anyone else – and I wouldn't let him, so there.'

'Well,' said Clare, in a trembling voice, 'people that do bad, unkind things always get punished for it. And I wouldn't be a bit surprised if something happens to your dog. But you can be sure if he comes to Francis he'll be well looked after!'

'You're talking nonsense,' said the boy, and he laughed. 'My dog's mine, I've had him for five years, and I'll never let him go. We've only just moved here – into one of the flats in that block – and though it's small and hasn't a garden like we used to have, Rex is quite happy, because he's with me. As for the silly pretend dog, take him – *I* don't want him!'

The boy bent down, pretended to pat a dog, and to undo a lead. 'You can go,' he said. 'I don't want you, Paddy.'

He made such a realistic little whine that Clare and Sam jumped. The boy laughed at them. 'Goodbye,' he said. 'And don't you go jumping too many people like that, little girl! I shall pull your hair hard if you jump on me again!'

'You won't,' said Sam, fiercely, speaking for the first time.

'I'll pull yours too, tiddler!' said the boy, and went off, still laughing. The two children stared after him. 'Horrid, horrid, hateful boy!' said Clare, and stamped her foot.

They ran to their front gate and went in. They went to find Francis and tell him what had happened. He stared in alarm.

'Clare! You *mustn't* do things like that! You're a *girl*! Girls don't behave like that. And you're a Brownie too!'

'I know lots of girls that would behave like that,' said

Clare defiantly. 'And a Brownie has to stick up for the right, hasn't she?'

'She was brave,' said Sam, in his slow solemn voice. 'Very brave. She wasn't a bit afraid of the big boy.'

'And he let Paddy go free, so he's yours again,' said Clare, trying to make Francis smile.

He shook his head. 'No. I told you the pretend had gone. It was a silly one. I'm too big to invent things now. Let's forget about it.'

'Where did your Paddy-dog sleep?' asked Sam, suddenly. 'I never heard you talking to him in our bedroom.'

'I cleaned out the old dog kennel,' said Francis. 'He slept there. Come and look. It's got straw inside and all!'

He took them to a corner of the garden, where the old dog kennel stood that Granny's dogs had slept in long ago. It was clean and spotless inside, and had a heap of straw there, flattened down as if a dog had actually slept on it. Outside stood a bowl of water.

'I never noticed the old kennel was cleaned out,' said Clare. 'Sam – come here! Look, Francis, he's getting into the kennel! *Sam!*'

Sam crawled right into the kennel, and then turned round and looked out, beaming. 'Woof,' he said, 'woof! I'm hungry. Get me a chocolate biscuit. Woooooof!'

Francis and Clare roared with laughter. Clare pulled Sam out and dusted the straw from his clothes.

'You're an idiot!' said Francis, suddenly looking cheerful. 'Now let's forget Paddy and never mention him again. I was silly.'

Clare suddenly remembered her news. 'Granny has been in a very good mood all day,' she said, 'and she has got us some chocolate biscuits for tea – loads of them. We'd better go in, else she'll forget her good mood and take the biscuits away! Come on.'

They all went indoors, and Francis explained that he couldn't help being late, because he was room monitor that week. Granny nodded approvingly.

'Then I know you'd do everything well,' she said. 'Your eye's looking better today, Francis. Have you seen that boy again, the one who fought you?'

Daddy cleared his throat warningly. 'Granny. No more is to be said about that.'

Clare kicked Sam under the table, and gave him a little secret smile. A good thing Daddy had said that – or poor Francis would have had to tell her about the afternoon's happenings over the wall!

Granny didn't like Daddy putting his foot down, and she frowned. Clare looked at her anxiously, hoping that nothing would happen before the chocolate biscuits were all eaten.

Mother changed the subject smoothly, a thing she was very good at. 'Has anyone counted the daffodils out in the dell yet?' she said. 'I counted twenty-nine yesterday. Remember that as soon as there are more than thirty we can pick some for the house. You'll do that, Clare, won't you?'

'Oh yes,' said Clare. She loved picking them and arranging them. Thank goodness Mother had changed the subject! 'I'll put some in Granny's room first, then in yours and Daddy's, and then in ours.'

'No, get some for the table first,' said Granny, pleasantly. 'Then we can all share them. Are you ready for a chocolate biscuit, Sam?'

'Ooooooh yes,' said Sam.

'Yes what?' asked Granny, holding the plate away from him.

'Oh – *please*. Thank you, Granny!'

'Manners, manners, manners,' said Granny. 'When I was little and forgot my Ps and Qs, my nurse cut out a whole lot of letters – all Ps and Qs – and pinned them on my frock. Each time I remembered she took one off – and each time I forgot she pinned one on.'

'Oh! How exciting!' said Clare. 'Granny, do do it to me! Please do!'

'It was a punishment,' said Granny. 'Not a treat. John, why are you laughing?'

She turned to Daddy, who was laughing loudly, a thing he didn't often do. Mother began to laugh too.

'We're only laughing because what you think was a punishment Clare wants for a treat,' she said. 'But Granny – it's only because Clare has good manners that she wants the Ps and Qs pinned on, she knows quite well that she wouldn't have the paper letters pinned on her for more than five minutes!'

'Did you have them on for hours and hours, Granny?' asked Sam, solemnly staring at her. Then Granny began to laugh too.

'I can't remember,' she said. 'Now – let's finish up the biscuits, shall we? They're so nice.'

After tea Clare went out into the garden to pick the daffodils. They were lovely. 'You're dancing!' said Clare. 'Do you like the wind, daffodils? Yes, you do, because you're nodding your heads at me!'

She counted them. There were fifty-three. 'Twenty-nine yesterday, fifty-three today,' she said. 'I can pick them all but thirty – how many's that?'

It was a nice big bunch. Clare picked some of the long green leaves too. She was just turning to go when she heard a voice.

'Hello!'

Clare stood still, startled. Where did the voice come from? She looked all round but couldn't see anyone. It came again, more urgently.

'Hello!'

'Where are you?' said Clare. 'I can't see you. Are you in the garden?'

'Yes. Here,' said the voice, and from behind a thick tangled mass of bushes stepped the boy. *The* boy – the one who had been in the fight with Francis, and who had been pummelled by Clare only an hour or so ago.

'What are you doing in our garden?' said Clare, at once. 'You're trespassing! Go away. I shall go and tell my mother at once if you don't!'

'No, listen,' said the boy. 'I'm not trespassing really. I want to speak to your brother – what's his name – Francis, isn't it? It's very urgent.'

'What do you want to speak to him about?' demanded Clare. 'I don't like you. You're a horrid boy. You go away or I'll yell for my mother.'

'No, please don't,' said the boy, and he came nearer. 'Please fetch your brother. *Please* do.'

Clare stared at him. His eyes were red. He was crying! A big boy like that! Whatever was the matter?

'I'll fetch Francis,' she said. 'Wait here.'

Clare ran off to find Francis, the daffodils still in her hands. What was that boy crying about? She had never seen such a big boy cry before. It seemed quite shocking. Even Sam hardly ever cried.

'Francis!' she called. 'Francis! Where are you?'

'He's up in his room,' said Granny. 'Don't shout so, Clare. You made me jump.'

Clare flew past Granny and past her father in his wheelchair. She ran upstairs to Francis's room. He was there getting ready his Scout uniform for a meeting next day.

Clare ran in and shut the door, panting. 'What's up?' said Francis, surprised.

'Francis – you know that big boy you fought – the one I jumped on this afternoon, who took Paddy away from you? Well, he's out in the dell and he wants you.'

'What for?' said Francis, with a scowl. 'Another fight?'

'No. He's crying,' said Clare, dropping her voice. Francis looked at her in surprise.

'Crying? What for? I bet he's not. He's too big!'

'He *is*, I tell you. I ordered him out of the garden, but he still kept on begging me to fetch you. I think he must be in trouble of some sort.'

'Well, he can't expect *me* to get him out of it,' said Francis grimly, getting up. 'I don't feel at all friendly towards him. All right – I'll go and see what he wants.'

'Shall I come too?' asked Clare.

'No. I'll call you if I want to. And warn Sam not to come butting in,' said Francis. 'I'll take him into the stables and see what he wants.'

He went downstairs. Clare followed him, and got a vase from the cupboard to put the daffodils in for the table. She wondered and wondered what the boy had come for. She simply couldn't imagine. She found Sam and told him. He couldn't imagine either.

Francis found the boy behind a bush at the back of the dell. He wasn't crying, but his eyes were still red. He smiled weakly at Francis when he saw him coming.

'What's up?' said Francis. 'I call it cheek of you to come here and send my sister for me.'

'It isn't really,' said the boy. 'Something awful's happened – and I thought you might help.'

'Come into the stables,' said Francis, and led the way. 'We'll be alone there. I can't think how I can help you, and I don't feel as if I want to.'

The boy went into the stables after Francis, and the door was shut behind them. 'Now,' said Francis. 'Tell me what's the matter.'

'It's my dog,' said the boy, and swallowed hard. 'My dog, Rex.' He stopped and couldn't go on.

'Well, what about your dog?' asked Francis. 'I don't see what your dog has to do with me. I don't feel *interested* in your dog after your behaviour to me.'

'I know. I'm sorry about that now,' said the boy. 'It was mean of me. But I've been punished for it – because my dog – my very own dog – is going to be taken away from me.'

'Not because of our fight!' said Francis, astonished.

'No. No one knows about that,' said the boy. 'Look, my name's Dan Oldham, and I live in one of the new flats in that big block not far off. And we've just been told that no one is allowed to keep pets in the flats. See?'

'Oh. So you can't keep Rex,' said Francis. 'That's bad luck!'

'Bad luck! It's worse than bad luck!' said Dan, and his eyes began to swell with tears again. 'He's going to be sent away for good, to my Uncle Tom. He doesn't like dogs, so old Rex will be chained up all day long, he'll never have a walk – and – and I expect they'll forget his water and won't give him enough straw, and . . .'

He couldn't say any more. He rubbed his hands over his eyes and turned away. 'I'm an idiot, I know,' he said. 'But I've had him for five years, and he's *mine*. Fancy never seeing him again, or feeling him lick me, or jump up at me to welcome me home! You've never had a dog of your own, so you don't know.'

'I can guess, though,' said Francis. 'How awful, Dan! Won't they really let you keep him?'

'No. My dad says we'll be turned out of the flat if we keep any pets. We didn't know that before we came. Well, Mum won't be turned out of her nice new flat – she waited for it for years. So Rex has got to go. I only heard this evening, just after I'd left that kid sister and brother of yours.' Dan sat down on a box and ran his hands through his mop of hair.

'Why did you come to me?' said Francis after a while.

'To ask you something. To *beg* you really,' said Dan. 'You love dogs, don't you? I know you do, because of that pretend dog you had. I'm terribly sorry I laughed at you now! Well – I want to know this – could you have my dog here for me? You've got a big garden, there's plenty of room. I'd bring his food for him, and take him for walks . . .'

Francis sat silent. Dan looked at him beseechingly. He put out his hand and touched Francis on the arm.

'You're a Scout. Have you done your good deed for today? This would be the very best good deed you ever did!'

Francis looked at him. 'I've done two good deeds today,' he said. 'But there's no reason why I shouldn't do a third, if . . .'

Dan leapt up in excitement, his eyes shining. 'Do you mean you'll have Rex?' he almost shouted.

'Sit down and listen,' said Francis. 'And don't get too excited, because I can't for the life of me see how we're going to manage a dog here. I don't believe Daddy would allow one. Mother would say he left dirty footmarks just when she had cleaned the floor . . .'

'But hasn't your mother got someone to help her in this big house?' said Dan. 'She doesn't do everything herself, does she?'

'*We* help, of course,' said Francis. 'But we're poor, because my father got hurt in the war and he can't work. And then there's my granny – now let me see. I don't know about Granny. She simply *loves* animals – but we had to send her dog Thumper away, because he was a Great Dane and ate too much, and it nearly broke her heart. She might not want another dog.'

'I see,' said Dan. 'Well – need we tell anyone? Rex is an *awfully* good dog. He won't bark unless burglars come, and you wouldn't mind that, would you? And I'll feed him and look after him, and everything, if you don't mind me coming into your garden. Honestly, Rex won't be a bit of a nuisance. You'll love him.'

'I expect I should,' said Francis, a little stir of excitement coming over him at the thought of a dog in the garden. 'If I *do* get to like him, I might want to take him for a few walks myself, Dan.'

There was a pause. 'Well,' said Dan at last, 'we could take him for walks together. Er – I'll pay you for keeping Rex for me, Francis. I get pocket money, but Mum pays for Rex's food. If I give you half my pocket money a week, that should be enough for you. I'll give you it all, of course, if it isn't.'

'I wouldn't want any pay,' said Francis, going red. 'I'm a Scout. I do good deeds for nothing. If you were a Scout you'd understand.'

'Golly!' said Dan. 'There's something in being a Scout if it makes you like that. Francis – are you going to *try* keeping Rex for me? I'll make it up to you somehow, I really will, even if you won't let me pay you in money. Come on.'

'I'm going to call Clare and Sam,' said Francis. 'I'll see

what they say.' He went out of the stables and shouted for his brother and sister. They came at once, for they had been hanging about hopefully near the stables.

Soon all four were having a great discussion. As soon as Clare and Sam heard of Dan's trouble they were on his side at once. Fights and quarrels were forgotten. Rex was the only thing that mattered.

'Of *course* we'll have Rex,' said Clare. 'Have you forgotten how you got that old kennel clean, and put straw in it, Francis?'

'No. I hadn't forgotten,' said Francis. 'It's almost as if it had been got ready for this very thing. It's right out of the way too – nobody ever goes into that part of the garden. We could put some wire round and make a kind of little yard, so that Rex wouldn't stray into the other part and give himself away.'

'Yes. We *must* keep this a secret,' said Clare. 'I don't believe Mother or Daddy or Granny would want Rex – for various reasons. He must be a secret. A secret! What a *lovely* secret! A dog of our own!'

'No,' said Dan at once. 'He'll still be mine, *all* mine. That's understood.'

'But we can share him, can't we?' said Clare. 'He sounds such a nice dog, Dan – you won't mind, surely, if we get fond of him?'

'Well – we'll see,' said Dan, jealously. 'Anyway, I can't stop you doing what you like. You're my only hope. And it's good of you to help me, considering how mean I was.'

'We've forgotten that,' said Francis. 'We don't ever need to mention it again.'

'I'm sorry I hit you so hard now,' said Dan. 'You must have had an awful eye.'

'I said forget it,' said Francis impatiently. 'Let's talk about when and how we're going to have Rex.'

'Could he come on Saturday?' asked Dan. 'That's when all dogs have to be out of the flats. I'll bring him then – and his own blanket and bowls. He'll be miserable at first, but if I tell him I'm coming next day and warn him not to whine, he'll be as good as gold.'

'Goodness, does he understand everything you say?' said Clare.

'Pretty well,' said Dan. 'It's a load off my mind, I can tell you. If ever I can do something in return I will.'

Rex was discussed in great detail. The three children felt as if they knew him very well indeed when they had heard all that Dan had to say about him.

'You know,' said Dan, at last, 'it's a very odd thing that your sister said to me this afternoon. "You be careful that your dog doesn't come to my brother!" And I laughed. But sure enough, it's happened.'

'Yes, it was funny I said that,' said Clare, looking startled. 'Very strange.'

Dan got up to go. He held out his hand solemnly to Francis. 'Thanks,' he said. 'I'll never forget this.'

'That's all right,' said Francis, and shook hands vigorously. Clare held out her hand, and then Sam held out his.

This rather solemn moment was broken suddenly by Granny's voice. 'Francis! Clare! Sam! Where in the world are you? Francis!'

'We must go,' said Francis. 'Stay here till we've gone indoors, then slip out home. See you on Saturday – and good luck, Dan!'

4

An Exciting Secret

The three children were so excited at the idea of keeping Dan's dog for him they could talk of nothing else when they were by themselves.

'Won't it be *lovely*?' said Clare. 'I know he'll still be Dan's dog, but he'll really seem like our own.'

'I hope it doesn't matter not telling anyone,' said Francis. 'But I can't see that we are doing anything but help someone in trouble. I wonder what Rex is like – Dan said he was a sort of spaniel.'

'I'll like him anyhow,' said Sam.

Granny put her head round the door of Clare's bedroom, where they were all sitting talking. 'What are you discussing up here so secretly?' she asked. 'Clare, your mother is doing the ironing – will you go and help her? A Brownie promises to help in the house, you know.'

Clare frowned. She did help in the house. In fact, she was very good in the house, doing plenty of jobs when she would much rather have been reading or playing. 'I'm coming, Granny,' she said, rather curtly.

'Well, you needn't say it like that,' said Granny, who seemed cross. 'I shouldn't have to come and fetch you.'

'You could have *called* me,' said Clare sulkily as she went out of the room. Oh dear, why did Granny always rub her up the wrong way? Granny was so very kind at heart, she would do anything for any of them – but she was always after them for something, especially Clare! Clare went slowly down the stairs, still frowning – but before she reached the bottom she began thinking about Dan's dog again, and she skipped the last three stairs in delight.

Great plans were being made by the three children. 'There's some wire netting in the stables,' said Francis. 'I *think* there's enough to make a kind of yard for the dog – big enough for him to run up and down in, anyway.'

'We'll need some posts to hold up the wire here and there,' said Clare. 'Have we got any?'

'Yes,' said Sam. 'I know where.' Sam knew where everything was. He knew every corner of the house and garden. When anyone wanted anything they always went to Sam.

'Good. Then you can find the posts and bring them,' said Francis. 'Good thing we've got the kennel – such a nice one too. Plenty of room for Rex.'

'Yes. And all cleaned out, with straw and everything ready!' said Clare. 'I'll give Rex fresh water every day. I'd like to do that.'

'No. That's my job,' said Francis at once. 'Remember, Dan asked *me* to look after Rex. I'm responsible for him.'

'Well – I expect *Dan* will want to give him his fresh water,' said Clare. 'He doesn't really want us to look after Rex, he's jealous that we should – but he's just got to let us because if we don't he'll lose him.'

'He can't give him water,' said Sam. 'The tap is in the scullery, and he'd be seen going in there.'

'Yes. That's true,' said Francis. They fell silent, thinking of all the things they might do for Rex. Sam began to whistle.

'Don't!' said Clare. 'Your whistle is dreadful, Sam. Why do you keep *on* whistling?'

'I was only whistling because I feel happy,' said Sam, looking hurt. 'I was whistling "It's a hap-hap-happy day".'

'Well, nobody would know it,' said Clare. 'It might just as well have been "God save the Queen". I wish you hadn't learnt to whistle, Sam. You drive Granny mad.'

'All right. I'll try not to,' said poor Sam. 'But it sort of comes whenever I feel specially happy.'

'Whistle, then,' said Francis, giving him a friendly punch. 'I know that feeling.'

'We ought to go and talk to Rex as much as we can,' said Clare. 'He'll be lonely without Dan.'

Everyone agreed heartily. 'I shall clean out his kennel,' said Sam firmly.

'You will not,' said Francis, just as firmly. 'That's my job.'

'Don't be mean. Take it in turns,' said Clare. 'As a Brownie, I think that's the right thing to do.'

'As a Cub, I agree,' said Sam, solemnly. They all laughed.

'This dog is going to be terribly spoilt,' said Francis. 'Wouldn't it be dreadful if he didn't like us?'

This was an awful thought. Clare changed the subject. 'We'll have to hope that none of the grown-ups discover Rex,' she said. 'It's a pity to have to keep him a secret from them – but it would be so dreadful if Rex was sent away to Dan's horrid uncle.'

'I'm going to find the wire netting,' said Francis, getting up. 'Mother and Granny are out. Only Daddy is in. It's a good moment to go.'

'Poor old Daddy. He'd like to join in this, I'm sure, and help to put up the wire,' said Clare. 'I wish his back would get better. I wish he was like other fathers, and could work and get about and enjoy things. He's so *patient*, sitting there always, watching other people rush about.'

'Yes, and each time the doctor thinks of some new treatment, he's as excited as we are about Rex – and then it comes to nothing, and he's back where he was,' said Francis.

'When I'm grown up,' said Sam, seriously, 'I'm going to be a doctor – a very clever one. And the first thing I'm going to do is to cure Daddy.'

'You've said that a hundred times,' said Clare. 'But I quite believe you. You hardly ever change your mind about anything, like I do. Do come on. Mummy will be back before we've done a thing.'

They got the wire netting, and Sam found the posts in the heap of junk in the harness room. They were just right. Francis got the pliers, and they dragged the wire and the posts to the distant corner of the big garden. It was right out of sight of the house, and as there was no path anywhere near it, it was a perfect spot to hide a dog. Bushes and trees screened the corner from view.

The kennel stood there, big and clean, straw sticking out of it. Sam rubbed his hands and began to whistle loudly. Clare laughed.

'Happy again?' she said. 'Get a move on, Sam. Francis will soon be ready for the posts. Untie them.'

The three children were very busy indeed for about an hour. The wire was unrolled and set up. Francis clipped it to size with the pliers. He forgot what sharp edges cut wire netting has, and got severely scratched on his right hand.

'You're bleeding!' said Sam. 'I'll get some ointment,' and he ran off on his short legs.

'Don't fuss!' shouted Francis.

'He's not fussing,' said Clare. 'Cuts like that ought to be cleaned out. If Rex cut his leg you'd clean it and put iodine on it, wouldn't you? Well, you're better than a dog! It won't take a minute.'

Sam came walking back. None of them ever ran when they were carrying bottles, it was such a silly thing to do. Granny had taught them that very thoroughly, and had shown them a terrible scar inside her right hand which had been caused by a piece of broken glass.

'I ran with a glass vase,' she said. 'I fell, and the vase broke and almost cut my hand in half. So don't you be silly, like me!'

Francis's hand was bound up with a bit of rag, and he went on with his work. Sam drove stakes into the wire at intervals, and the netting held up nice and straight.

There was just enough to go all round the piece they had chosen for the dog-run.

It looked good when it was finished. There was no gate, but the wire was low enough for them all to jump over, though Sam could only just clear it. It was quite high enough to keep a dog in – unless it was a dog that could jump very well indeed.

Francis pulled all the straw out of the kennel and then put it back again. 'You flattened it down terribly, Sam, when you got into the kennel,' he said. 'A dog likes nice loose straw he can cuddle into.'

'He'll flatten it down just as I did,' said Sam.

'We can make his bed freshly each day,' said Clare. 'I wish it was Saturday!'

Saturday came at last – and with it came Dan, leading Rex, his dog. He came in at the back gate, where all three children were waiting for him in excitement.

'Hello!' said Dan, who looked extremely serious; but then it *was* serious business to hand over a dog in this way. 'Rex – shake paws!'

Rex held out his right paw, and shook hands solemnly with Francis, then with Clare, then with Sam. Sam shook it and shook it and shook it. Rex didn't seem to mind.

'That's enough,' said Dan. 'Don't shake his paws off. Well – what do you think of him?'

The children looked at Rex admiringly. He was certainly a *sort* of spaniel, but not quite. He was a bit too big, and his tail was too long – but he had the beautiful melting brown eyes of the true spaniel, and the long, drooping, silky ears. He looked up at the children and wagged his tail vigorously.

'He's beautiful!' said Clare, and dropped down on her knees to pet him.

'He's a real dog!' said Francis, and patted the silky coat. 'A proper *doggy* kind of dog!'

'I like him very much,' said Sam. 'Very, very, very much.'

Dan looked as if he was about to burst with pride and delight.

'I'm glad,' he said gruffly and patted Rex. 'He's not bad, and he's as good as gold. Er – I think you're awfully decent kids, all of you. I do really!'

Nobody answered. Rex was taking all their attention. Pleased at so much fussing he rolled over on his back and pedalled his legs in the air, as if he was riding a bicycle with four pedals!

'Look at him!' said Clare, and tickled him.

Dan began to talk to Francis, telling him all his arrangements. 'I told my mum,' he said. 'She wasn't very pleased at first – Rex going to strangers. But I begged her so hard that she gave in. She thinks it's jolly decent of you.'

'We shall love to have him,' said Francis. 'What about his food? Will you bring it every day or what?'

'Yes. I'll come and feed him,' said Dan. 'And I'll come and take him for a walk whenever I can. But you will have to give him fresh water – do you mind?'

'We'd love to,' said Francis. 'I say – haven't you kept him well? His coat is like silk, and even his ears are brushed.'

'Yes, and his feathers too,' said Dan proudly.

'Oh, where are his feathers?' said Sam, looking Rex all over in surprise. 'I thought he only had hair.'

'The shaggy hair at the back of his legs is called "feathers",' said Dan, with a laugh. 'Well, I must go. Goodbye, Rex, old boy. Be good. I'll come and see you this evening!'

The back gate slammed. Dan was gone. Rex stood listening, and gave a little whine. Where was his beloved master?

'It's all right,' said Francis, and patted him. But Rex didn't think so. He ran at the wire and found that he couldn't get out. He ran all round, but found no opening. He sat down and whined again.

The children made a fuss of him, afraid that he might bark. But he didn't. He suddenly got up and walked to the kennel, looked at it with interest. He went right inside and sniffed round. The children could hear his sniffs quite well. They sounded quite pleased sniffs.

There was a little thud – and Rex peeped out of the kennel. He had flopped down on the straw, and was now looking out of the entrance, master in his own little house.

'He likes it! He knows it's his,' said Sam, in delight. 'Look at him!'

They all gazed at Rex, who looked at them out of his trusting brown eyes. Then he suddenly got up, walked out of his kennel and licked first Francis, and then Sam, then Clare. Then he went to his water bowl and drank noisily.

'He ought to have something to eat,' said Clare. 'He's got nothing he can nibble at if he feels hungry. What about a chocolate biscuit, Francis? I've got one in my room that I saved up.'

'No, certainly not,' said Francis at once. 'Chocolate will make him fat. He's going to be fed properly, like a dog. And I think we ought to let Dan feed him; not even give him snacks ourselves. It wouldn't be fair.'

'I would like to buy him a bone to gnaw,' said Sam. 'I'll ask Dan.'

'Oh dear – I suppose we ought to leave Rex and go back to the house,' said Clare. 'You've got a Scouts' meeting this morning, haven't you, Francis? And I've got to help Mummy. Sam, you've got to run the errands.'

'I know,' said Sam. 'But Mother said not till half-past ten. It isn't that yet. You two go. I'll stay with Rex till half-past ten, in case he's lonely.'

The other two didn't much like leaving Sam alone with the spaniel. It might be more friendly with him than with them! Still – it would be nice for Rex to have company for a little while. So the two elder ones went off together. They heard Sam beginning to whistle very loudly indeed.

'Sam's happy,' said Clare. 'Hear him whistling! Isn't Rex *nice*, Francis? Isn't it exciting to have a secret like this?'

They went happily to their jobs, hugging their secret, longing for a minute to spare to rush down to the spaniel.

Mother was wondering where they were. 'I've called and called!' she said. 'Where were you?'

'In the garden,' said Francis. 'Sorry, Mother.'

'What *were* you doing?' said Granny. 'I couldn't find even one of you!'

Francis and Clare didn't know what to answer to that, so they said nothing. They did hope that Granny wouldn't poke and probe into their secret. Mother never did that. But dear old Granny couldn't seem to rest unless she knew everyone's thoughts and doings.

Certainly Granny grew very curious that day as first Clare disappeared when her jobs were done, and then when Sam had done the errands, he disappeared too. When Francis came back from his Scouts' meeting just before dinner, he changed into ordinary things – and then he disappeared as well!

'Where are they?' wondered Granny. 'Now they've *all* gone!'

'Let them be,' said Daddy. 'It's a lovely day. I expect they've got some secret out in the garden – building a little house, or climbing some tree. They've done their jobs, and done them well. Let them alone, Granny.'

'*Well*! Anyone would think I was always after them, to hear you talk!' said Granny. 'They're my grandchildren, aren't they? And they're living in my house, aren't they? Can't I wonder where they are?'

'I wish you'd sell the house and let us go into a smaller one!' said Daddy wearily. 'All that work for my poor wife – and the children too. We'd have a much easier time in a small house. It's dreadful to sit here and watch you all slaving yourselves to death!'

Tears began to run down Granny's cheeks. She went over to Daddy and patted his hand. 'Poor boy,' she said.

'I know it's hard for you – but maybe the doctors will get you right one day, and then you'll be glad we kept this nice house and garden! It was my childhood home, and I lent it to you when you married my daughter, and it would break my heart to sell it and go.'

'Yes, I understand,' said Daddy. '*You* do more than you should, too – I know that. But I can't bear watching you all doing things and not being able to help at all, except peel apples and potatoes and shell the peas! It makes me cross, it makes us all on edge with each other. A family should live in unity and peace and kindliness. Sometimes we don't.'

Granny wiped her eyes and made up her mind to go straight out that afternoon and buy sweets for the children, new stockings for their mother, and some cigarettes for their father.

'I'm a bad old woman,' she said. 'Cross and pernickety and nagging. Aren't I, Mr Black?'

The enormous black cat had come gliding into the room, his yellow eyes shining. He leapt straight up into the little old lady's arms, and purred loudly.

'You and that cat!' said Daddy, smiling. 'He's the only person who never aggravates you, Granny!'

Granny squeezed Mr Black a little and he gave a small squeal and struggled to get down. Mother came into the room and looked round. 'Where *are* the children?' she said. 'Don't say they've disappeared again!'

They disappeared continually for the next week! It was arranged that out of school hours one of them should always be with Rex, if possible. He didn't bark, but he did whine if he knew the children were in the house. They were terribly afraid that somebody would hear him.

Dan came regularly every day, and took Rex for a long walk. The dog went nearly mad when he heard and saw him coming, but he never once barked. Dan had warned him not to and the intelligent creature understood.

Dan brought him meat each day, and biscuits. He inspected the water bowl to see that completely fresh water had been put into it. It always had. Francis made it one of the first jobs of his day.

One morning Dan saw that the kennel had been shifted round, and was now facing in another direction. 'Why have you moved the kennel?' he asked. 'It looks funny facing that way.'

'Well,' said Francis, 'we've been having some very cold east winds the last two days, and Rex's kennel was facing east, so the wind blew straight in. And I couldn't help thinking how cold it must be to lie in a draughty east wind each night – so I shifted the kennel round. Now he ought to be nice and snug at night.'

'You're a good friend to him,' said Dan gratefully. 'Doesn't he look well? He's happy too, isn't he? Though I think he misses me awfully.'

'Oh, he does,' said Francis. 'Everytime anyone comes in at the back gate, he stands listening, hoping it's you. But he's quite happy. We all love him.'

'Could you take him for a walk tomorrow?' said Dan. 'I've got to go with my mother and visit my granny, and I won't be able to come after tea and take him out. But he must have his walk.'

Francis's eyes shone. 'Oh yes. I'd love to take him. I never thought you'd let me. I say, doesn't it make a difference having a dog? I can't *think* what we did without Rex – always someone to pet and talk to and play with. And, you know, when I did the wrong homework the other day, and got kept in for an hour, I was jolly miserable – and Rex seemed to know, and he made a terrific fuss of me when I went to see him.'

'Well, all dogs are like that,' said Dan. 'They always take your side, you know – rather like mothers do. All right then; I'll come and feed him tomorrow, but you'll take him for his walk. Thanks!'

It was a real thrill for the children to go out with Rex. Granny was as inquisitive as ever when they said they all wanted to go off together for a walk. She even wanted to come too, and was quite upset when they politely said no, they were going too far for Granny.

They set off when they thought no one at the house was looking. They put Rex on his lead until they got out into the lanes. Then they slipped him off. He raced off madly and for one awful moment the children thought he wasn't coming back. 'He won't go to try and find Dan, will he?' asked Clare.

'Rex! Heel!' called Francis. And the well-trained dog came back at once, and walked just behind him, his nose almost touching Francis's heel. It reminded him of Paddy, the dog he had invented only a little while ago. Francis laughed at himself.

'How silly I was! Still, he was better than nothing, even if he was only a shadow dog. Here, Rex – fetch this stick!'

They had a wonderful time with Rex, and they were all tired out when they got back for tea. Rex flopped down in his kennel with an enormous sigh, and put his silky head on his feet, his long ears spread out beside his head.

'I feel like that too, Rex,' said Sam, 'all floppy. I'm awfully hungry. I hope Granny won't ask us *too* many questions about our walk. I feel I might be silly and say something about Rex.'

'You jolly well won't!' said Clare, in horror. 'You'll get the biggest kick under the table that you ever got in your life if you do!'

Dan turned up the next day, beaming. 'Did he like his walk? He says he did! Look, I've got something for you all. I bought them out of my pocket money. You wouldn't take any payment for looking after Rex, but I've got to do *something*!'

He held out a tin of boiled sweets. 'Oh! How *nice* of you!' said Clare. 'But – we want to look after Rex for love, not for payment.'

'Go on, take them,' said Dan. 'My mum said I ought to bring you sweets every week if you won't let me pay you.'

'Well – we'll take them this week, thank you very much,' said Francis. 'But only this once, see? We *want* to look after Rex for nothing. We all like to do it for our good deeds, as well as because we like Rex.'

'I never met kids like you before,' said Dan. 'Doing something for nothing! Most people want all they can get. Well, I'm glad you'll take the sweets this week. They're the best I could get for you. Don't give Rex any, will you? He's got beautiful teeth, and I don't want them spoilt.'

'Things are going very well,' said Francis, handing the tin of sweets round. 'Very well indeed. Granny has given up asking where we disappear to – and I don't think our secret will ever be found out!'

But that was rather a silly thing to say. Because, the very next week, it *was* found out!'

5

A Bit of Good Luck

Granny found out about Rex first. It was all because of Mr Black, her cat. He often went bird-watching, and was always most annoyed because as soon as he got within pouncing distance of a bird, it at once flew up into the air, sat on a bough, and sang rude things at him.

Mr Black didn't like that. He wasn't at all good at bird-catching, fortunately, because he was too big and heavy to run fast – and also he was very easily seen. The birds always set up a great clamour when they saw him in the garden.

'Look out, look out! The cat's about!' sang the thrush.

'Beware, beware. The cat is here!' fluted the blackbird.

'Pimm-im-im-im! I see him-im-im-im!' called the bluetit who was nesting in the orchard.

One morning, when the children were at school, Mr Black went bird-hunting again. He saw a fat blackbird, and stalked him warily, keeping behind bushes, never once treading on a twig or a rustling leaf. He was as good as a Red Indian!

The blackbird led him a fine dance, hopping on well ahead. He led him right down to where Rex's yard was.

Then he flew up into a tree and called Mr Black such dreadful names that Mr Black couldn't bear it. He leapt right up into the tree as high as he could after the cheeky bird.

The blackbird flew away. Mr Black sat down on the bough and began to wash himself. He always did that when a bird or mouse had got the better of him. It was just to show the world that *he* didn't care, anyway!

He heard a noise down below and looked to see what made it. What he saw down there made him swell up to twice his size, and the fur on his tail swelled too, so that Mr Black was a truly ferocious sight.

What he saw was Rex, the spaniel, lying down in the sun fast asleep. A dog! A dog in Mr Black's own garden! How dare he!

Mr Black hissed and spat. Rex woke up with a jump. Birdsong and bird calls never disturbed him – but the unusual spitting, hissing noise woke him up at once.

He leapt up and looked round, growling. Mr Black spat again, and Rex looked up. He was amazed to see such an enormous black creature in the tree above his kennel. *Was* it a cat? He had never seen such a big one before.

He growled again. Mr Black hissed. He didn't dare to get down for he didn't realize that Rex was penned in; he was afraid that the dog would catch him as he slid down the tree trunk.

So Mr Black sat up there, hissing and spitting, and Rex got more and more excited, running round his pen, trying to find a way out so that he could jump up against the tree trunk near by.

He forgot that he mustn't bark. He gave a small bark and then a louder one. Then he got so excited that he almost barked the place down, and Mr Black determined to stay up the tree for weeks, if necessary, rather than face this fierce dog.

Granny was alone in the house. Mother had gone to the shops and had taken Daddy in his wheelchair. Granny didn't take any notice of the barks at first. Then, as they went on and on, louder and louder, more and more excited, she sat up and frowned.

'Where is that barking dog?' she said. 'What a dreadful noise! Who keeps a dog that barks like that? I really must complain. And where is Mr Black? He usually comes rushing in if he hears a dog bark. Mr Black! Mr Black, where are you?'

But as Mr Black was high up in the oak tree over the kennel, he didn't come. Granny called again and again, and all the while she could hear Rex barking madly.

'Oh! I *hope* it's not Mr Black he's barking at!' she thought, suddenly. 'I must go and see.' So out into the garden she went, in the direction of the barks. And, of course, she came to the dog-run at the bottom of the garden, where Rex was barking his head off! She didn't see Mr Black at first. She was so astonished to see a dog in a little yard, with a kennel, that she had eyes for nothing else!

'A dog!' she said. 'A dog penned up in the yard here! So *that's* where the children have been disappearing to for the last week or so – they've come down here to the dog.

What an *extraordinary* thing! Wherever did they get the dog? And why didn't they tell anybody?'

Rex saw Granny. He stopped barking and looked at her. He ran to the netting and stood against it, his forepaws pressing the wire. He whined. He felt sure this old lady liked animals.

Granny put her hand over the wire and patted his silky head. 'What lovely eyes you have!' she said. 'Real spaniel eyes. What are you doing here?'

'Woof,' said Rex, and wagged his tail.

'How do I get into your yard?' wondered Granny. 'There's no gate. I suppose the children just jump over. Well, I can climb over somehow, I suppose.'

Then she suddenly saw Mr Black – and heard him too, because he gave a loud wailing yowl that startled Granny very much. 'Oh, so *there* you are!' she said, looking up into the tree. '*That's* where you've got to! Stalking birds again, I suppose, and came too near this dog. You can get down – the dog can't get you.'

Granny somehow managed to climb over the wire netting, and got into the little yard. Rex flung himself on her as if she were a long-lost friend. He licked her, and fussed round her, and whined. Anybody would have thought he was Granny's dog!

'You're a good dog,' she said, patting him. 'It's a long time since I had a dog. Well, well, well – I can't get over this! Do you *belong* to the children?'

'Woof,' said Rex, and lay on his back to be tickled – and just as Granny was bending over him, tickling him and making him squirm in delight, the children came home! They did what they always did; ran to see if Rex was all right.

And goodness gracious, there was Granny in the little yard, bending over Rex, and tickling him and talking to him. *Granny!*

They stopped in amazement. Rex heard them and leapt up, running to the wire to welcome them. He loved these children!

'Granny!' said Clare. 'Oh, Granny! You've found Rex!'

'Yes,' said Granny, looking quite guilty. 'He barked at Mr Black – up there in the tree – and I came to see what the matter was. Whose dog is he? Yours?'

'Granny, are you cross about it?' asked Sam, jumping over the wire and going up to her. 'It's our secret. We didn't tell *you* because we thought you might not want any dog after your Thumper had had to be sent away. We didn't tell Mother because we thought she wouldn't like a dog racing about and messing the floors with muddy feet. And we didn't tell Daddy because it might worry him.'

'I see,' said Granny. 'I understand all that. But whose dog *is* he? You haven't told me yet. Is he yours?'

Then the whole thing had to come out. Clare and Francis told their secret, standing in the yard with Granny, while Rex and Sam played with one another and listened.

'Granny, *dear* Granny, please keep our secret,' begged Clare, earnestly, when she had finished her story. 'You can see how important it is to Dan, can't you? He loves Rex like you loved Thumper.'

'But Mother might not mind at all,' began Granny, and then, as she saw the look on the children's faces, she nodded her head. 'All right. Don't look like that. I know that's it's only to save your mother worry and bother that you want your secrèt kept. I won't be a spoilsport! I'll keep it!'

She was almost swept off her feet by three grateful children and Rex, who thrilled with the sudden excitement of his friends, flung himself on Granny with the rest. Granny began to laugh.

'Oh, set me free! You're choking me! I do promise you this – that as long as Rex is happy here and doesn't make a noise, I'll keep your secret. But Mother may quite well come down to this bit of the garden some time, you know, and find out for herself!'

'She never comes down here,' said Sam. 'She doesn't like this part. She says it's so untidy.'

Granny was really just as thrilled as the children about Rex. She went to visit him when they were at school. She bought him a very big bone, which he at once buried in the depths of his kennel, in case Mr Black should see it. She made such a fuss of him that it was just as well he was a good well-trained dog, or he would have been quite spoilt!

Dan wasn't very pleased that Granny knew, nor was he very pleased when he heard that she was giving him bones! '*I* want to feed him,' he said. 'His straw will get full of bones! And who's been brushing him? I do that, you know.'

'Well, we all do it, actually,' said Clare. 'He's so nice to brush and he does love it so. Granny bought him a brush yesterday – a nice scratchy one that he loves.'

'You should hear Sam when he brushes him,' said Francis, with a sudden giggle. 'He whistles *all* the time just as if he were grooming a horse! On and on and on, without any tune at all.'

'I don't,' said Sam. 'I have a tune. You're mean about my whistling.'

'Do you suppose Rex is safe, now your granny knows?' said Dan. 'Grown-ups do sometimes give things away, you know – to one another, I mean.'

'Oh yes, he's safe enough. Mother will never guess!' said Clare. 'I tell you she never comes down here, and Granny has *promised* not to tell – and she always keeps her word, always.'

Mother did wonder why Granny kept disappearing, though. She had got used to the children disappearing and thought nothing of it now – but she kept missing Granny! Whenever she went to ask her something Granny wasn't there. She wasn't anywhere in the house!

'Dear me – she must have got very fond of the garden all of a sudden,' thought Mother. But she didn't go down to see what the old lady was doing. Mother never interfered with anyone, and she was glad that Granny seemed so happy these days.

In fact, it is quite possible that she would never, never have found out about Rex if something rather extraordinary hadn't happened one morning. Mother was in the kitchen making a pudding when there came a knock on the back door.

'If that's the laundry, just bring it in,' called Mother. 'My hands are all floury.'

The door opened – but it wasn't the laundry. It was a small, pleasant-faced woman who Mother didn't know.

'Excuse me,' she said. 'I'm Dan's mother, and I've come to say thank you very much for letting your children look after his dog for him.'

Well! Mother stared at her in amazement. 'What *do* you mean?' she said. 'A dog? *I've* never heard of one! I think you must have made a mistake!'

The woman at the door looked as surprised as Mother. 'But – this *is* Green Meadows, isn't it?' she said. 'And you *are* Mrs Marshall, aren't you – the mother of Francis, Clare and Sam?'

'Yes,' said Mother, even more surprised. 'But how do you know about us? And what is this about a dog? There isn't one here! I ought to know!'

'Oh,' said the woman. 'Well, I'm Mrs Oldham, Dan's mother, who owns the dog. He told me all about your three. He once had a fight with your Francis, I think – and then somehow they made friends over the dog, and when my Dan was told he couldn't have his dog in our flat, he was upset; and he came to ask your Francis if he'd look after him in your big garden.'

'And did Francis say he would?' asked Mother, more and more astonished. 'I've not heard a word about this. But dear me – perhaps that's why the children keep disappearing. They go to look after the dog. But why didn't they tell me? It's not like them to do something behind my back.'

'Well, Mrs Marshall – I'll tell you what my son said about keeping the dog down the garden,' said Mrs Oldham, and she came right into the kitchen. 'He said that your three didn't want you to be *worried* with a dog in the house, running about dirtying the floors – he said you'd nobody to help you to clean or cook, and the children didn't want to give you any more trouble; and a dog *is* a trouble and a nuisance sometimes. So they put him at the bottom of the garden. But Dan never told me you didn't know.'

Mother took all this in, still full of astonishment. 'Let's go down the garden and see if we can find this dog,' she said. So, floury hands and all, she led the way down the garden, followed by Mrs Oldham.

And there, in the little yard, was Rex – and dear me, with him was Granny, brushing him vigorously with the new brush she had bought. Rex was loving it.

'Granny!' said Mother, amazed. 'So *you* knew about the dog! And you kept it from me too. I really don't know *what* to say!'

Rex nearly went mad when he saw Dan's mother. He thought she had come to fetch him back home to the flat, and he tried his hardest to jump over the wire netting. Mrs Oldham leaned over and patted him. 'You do look well!' she said. 'All silky and shiny. My, you've found some good friends!'

The three women began to talk, and soon Mother knew everything. 'A dog in the garden and I never knew,' she said. 'Those children!'

'Don't be cross with them,' begged Mrs Oldham.

'They did it out of the kindness of their hearts, to help my Dan. And do you know, they won't let him pay them a penny for looking after the dog and giving him the kennel and all! Not a penny. Dan says they won't even let him give them sweets now.'

'No, I don't expect they will,' said Mother. 'They've been taught not to want payment for any kindness they do.'

'Well, now, look here,' said Mrs Oldham, a sudden firmness coming into her voice. 'Two can think that way! You won't take anything for doing a kindness; well, I won't accept a kindness without doing one in return. Fair's fair, isn't it?'

Mother laughed. 'Yes, that's fair enough. I understand that. I like to return a kindness too.'

'Good,' said Mrs Oldham. 'Now will you let me do you a kindness, then? Just to make things square between us?'

'What sort of kindness?' asked Mother cautiously.

'I'll tell you,' said the little woman, beaming. 'I haven't got enough to do in my little flat – so I go out and work in other people's houses now and again. For money, of course, because that's work. And I'd like to come to you for a morning a week, and do anything you want me to do – for *nothing*, because that would be a pleasure, and I'd feel I was returning your kindness.'

'Oh no!' said Mother. But Granny interrupted.

'Oh yes!' she said, feeling a great liking for this pleasant-faced woman. 'Oh *yes*! What a wonderful thing it would be for you to have one whole morning a week free – you're working all day long every day of the week. Yes, Mrs Oldham, we accept with pleasure, it's a very kind thought of yours.'

And before Mother could say another word, the two of them had fixed it up together. Mrs Oldham would come every Wednesday – and yes, she would do the whole of the kitchen – and dear me, of course she could do a bit of cooking – and she could go over all the rooms too! That was nothing!

They all went back to the house, feeling pleasantly excited. Rex whined when he saw them go – but very soon the children were home and he greeted them joyfully, trying to tell them of all the visitors he had had that afternoon.

They ran up to the house for dinner. Mother was just finishing her preparations because she had got very behind. She looked up smiling.

'Hallo, dears! Would you like to take this bone down to Rex?'

The three children stared, completely taken aback. *What* had Mother said? She laughed. 'All right – I know your secret! Mrs Oldham came this morning, and I soon found out everything. It was sweet of you not to want to worry me, but Rex won't bother me a bit. You can let him come into the house whenever you want to. He's a very nice dog.'

Well, what a tremendous surprise! Sam flung himself on his mother. 'Oh Mother, I do love you! You always say the right things. Can I go and get Rex now, this very minute, at once?'

'Yes, now, this very minute, at once, if not sooner!' said Mother, and everyone laughed to see Sam's feet twinkling fast down the garden path.

Rex was a great success in the house. He made friends with Daddy, at once, and soon learnt not to lean too heavily against his legs. Granny loved having him about, and Mother didn't seem to mind at all, not even when his feet *were* muddy!

Sam tried to teach Rex to wipe his feet, and spent ages lifting up one foot afer another, wiping each one carefully on the mat. But Rex just wouldn't learn!

Clare was pleased to hear that Mrs Oldham was coming in a whole morning each week to help. She knew better than the boys, what that meant to her mother. And Mrs Oldham proved to be the greatest help possible. She didn't mind *what* she did, and often she came popping in to say she was going to town to the shops, could she fetch anything for Mother?

The only person who couldn't bear Rex coming into the house was Mr Black. He was very dignified about it, but he liked to give Rex a good slap if he came too near – and he hated to see Granny making a fuss of the spaniel.

'Mr Black's sulking again!' Clare would say. 'Look, Granny, he's turned his back on you. Mr Black, turn round.'

But Mr Black wouldn't. He sat there haughtily, his back to everyone, and wouldn't turn round at all until somebody said 'Dinner'. Then he looked round quickly.

Dan came to tea the next week, very clean and well-brushed and neat. 'You do look tidy,' said Sam.

'I've never seen you like this before.'

'Well – my mum's always going on at me because I don't look like you do,' said Dan. 'She thinks the world of your family. She thinks your mother's the best!'

To say that anyone was the best was the highest compliment Dan could pay. The children were pleased. *They* knew that their mother was the best, but it was nice to hear someone else say so.

Dan enjoyed coming to tea very much, but he was disappointed when Francis had to leave immediately afterwards to go to a Scout meeting. He gazed at him enviously.

'You do look good, all rigged up like that, badges and all. Can I try on your hat?'

He tried it on and looked at himself in the glass. He gave it back to Francis. 'I wish I was coming too,' he said.

'Well, why don't you?' said Francis, surprisingly. 'Why don't you become a Scout? We want a few more in my patrol. We could do with someone like you.'

'Gosh!' said Dan. 'I never thought of being a Scout myself! I'll come along. They won't mind at the meeting, will they, if I come?'

So off he went with Francis. They took Rex with them, and he was delighted. He was always wildly happy to see Dan, and never really considered himself to be anyone else's dog, though the three children did their best to make him belong to them as well.

He loved having the free run of Green Meadows. Two or three times he had run off and disappeared, but he always came back sooner or later. He just ran off to Dan's flat when he felt homesick – but when Dan or Mrs Oldham sent him back again, he went quite obediently.

'He's really got *two* homes,' said Sam to Dan, and Dan agreed.

One day Dan brought a girl about his age to see Francis and Clare. 'This is Rita,' he said. 'She's come to live in the flat next door. She's got a kitten – and, of course, we mustn't have even kittens in our flats. Could you have her kitten till she gets a home for it? Her mother will pay for its food and milk.'

'But what will Mr Black say?' said Clare. 'He might go for it.'

'I was wondering if you could keep it in the stables,' said Dan. 'You told me that once upon a time, when your granny's father kept horses there, there were so many stable cats she couldn't keep count of them – so it must be a good place for a cat.'

Francis laughed. He called his mother. 'Mother! Here's another refugee wanting a home – a kitten. Can we keep it in the stables?'

Rita had said nothing at all. She was pale and thin, with eyes much too large for her small face. Mother looked at her, thinking that she wanted a lot of fresh air and sunshine!

'If we have your kitten, will you come two or three times a day and feed it and pet it?' she said. 'And take it for little walks round the garden with you?'

'I'd love to,' said Rita, almost in a whisper. 'It's – it's the first pet I've ever had.'

'Well – we'll have it here till you can find a home for it,' said Mother. 'We all love animals here, you know.'

'Thank you very much,' said Rita. 'I'll bring it tomorrow.'

So a kitten came to join the family at Green Meadows. Rex gave it a great welcome, and it loved him, after its first fright at seeing such a big dog. But Mr Black didn't make friends so easily. Mother said it would be just as well not to bring the kitten into the house at all, until it had grown bigger, in case Mr Black flew at it.

So it lived quite happily in the stables, and was named Dapple, after the name on one of the brass plates there. It was a good name for it, for it was dappled all over – brown and black and white.

'We're getting quite a menagerie!' said Clare, pleased. 'I wonder what will come next.'

6

Flash the Pony

The kitten grew quickly. It escaped from the stables one day and went to the house, mewing for milk. Rita hadn't arrived yet with its food, and it was hungry.

It crept in at the kitchen door. Nobody was there. It saw a fire glowing in the grate and it padded over to it. It lay down on the rug.

At that very moment Mr Black stalked into the room. *His* place was also on the rug. He stopped and stared at the little bundle of fur lying there quite still. He sniffed delicately – dear me, it smelt like cat!

He put out a paw and touched the little ball of fur. The kitten awoke and leapt up. It saw Mr Black, and thought the big cat wanted to play. So he darted all round him, playfully, patting his waving tail, and making little rushes at him.

Mr Black was most astonished at all this. It was a long, long time since he had seen a kitten, and he wasn't quite sure what this little bit of quicksilver was. He put out a big paw and tried to pat it – but the kitten was away at once. Mr Black followed. Memories of his own mad kittenhood stirred in him, and he wanted to play with this funny little thing.

Granny had the surprise of her life when she came in and found Mr Black trying to squeeze his huge body under the armchair to get at the kitten, which kept putting out a paw and smacking him on his nose.

'Well, Mr Black! You've not played like this since you were a kitten yourself!' said Granny, in delight. 'Who would have thought you would make friends with that little rascal of a kitten?'

After that, of course, there really wasn't any need to keep the kitten shut up in the stables. It became one of the family too. Rita came faithfully each day with fish and milk, and sometimes she brought a little ball or a bit of ribbon. She took Dapple out into the sunshine to play, and the sunshine did her as much good as it did the kitten!

Daddy loved the kitten. He said it made him feel better just to watch it. It chased its own tail endlessly, it went mad regularly every evening after tea, tearing round and round the room at top speed, tail in air, and it dribbled a ball along the floor twenty times a day.

'It would make a very good footballer!' said Daddy. 'I never saw anyone dribble a ball so well.'

One night something happened. Francis woke up to see a curious light in the sky. What could it be? He jumped out of bed to find out. He looked through the window and saw that there was a fire somewhere.

'I must dress,' he thought. 'I'm a Scout, and I ought to go and see if I can help. I can at least fill buckets of water till the fire brigade comes.'

He was soon out of doors. He didn't wake anyone else.

It would only worry Mother and Granny to see the fire, and Daddy couldn't possibly go and help. Rex whined to go with him, but Francis shut his ears to Rex for once, as he passed near the kennel.

The fire was at the back of the greengrocer's shop. People were milling about there in a crowd, shouting and trying to help. The fire engine hadn't arrived.

'The sheds that the greengrocer uses for his stores and for his delivery boys' bicycles are on fire,' said a man. 'Goodness knows how it happened, this fire. The greengrocer was taken to hospital today, and his wife's spending the night there with him, he's so bad.'

'Nobody's in the shop part at all then?' said a woman. 'Well, we must try and save it from burning down – it's bad enough that old Miller's sheds should be burnt down, and him in hospital too!'

A man went by dragging a garden hose. Francis ran to help him. Buckets of water were being passed up by a chain of helpers, and the sizzling of water on flames was very loud. A horrible smell of smoke was blown over Francis, and he choked.

He ran out of the smoke, coughing. And then he heard a noise that went right through his heart.

It was the sound of a horse, whinnying in terror! A horse! Where was it? Not in the sheds, surely?

Francis ran to the chain of helpers. 'I heard a horse whinnying. Is there one anywhere? Quick, tell me!'

'Why, that would be little Flash the pony,' said the man. 'We forgot all about him. I reckon old Miller kept him in one of these sheds. Poor little thing!'

Francis flew off at once, his heart beating fast. He heard the whinnying again, and ran in the direction it came from. It seemed to come from the last shed of all, where hungry flames were just licking the roof, reaching out from a shed near by.

Francis went to the shed. Yes, the pony must be inside. He heard the frantic sound of hooves as the animal ran round and round the shed, banging into the sides. It whinnied in panic.

When Francis found that the pony's door was locked, he began to rain blows on the old wooden door with a stick. Some of the strips of wood broke, and Francis tore them out. The flames came nearer, and the boy panted as he struck the door again and again.

A man came up to help. He was big and strong, and he soon broke the door down. Francis pushed himself inside while the man went on making the hole bigger. He found the pony very quickly, because the frightened creature ran right into him, almost knocking him over.

Francis caught its mane and held on tightly. He called soothingly to the little thing. 'It's all right, I've got you safe. Come out with me.'

Somehow, he never quite knew how, he got the pony out of the broken-down doorway. He held on tightly to its mane, for the little creature was frantic, and it was only its fear of leaving this boy that stopped it from bolting.

Francis led the pony right away from the fire, and made it stand still. It was trembling from head to foot. Francis couldn't see what it was like in the dark, he only knew that it was small and had a long thick mane.

He stroked and patted the velvety nose, and spoke in his low, calm voice, saying all sorts of nonsense – but nonsense or not, the pony seemed to understand, and quietened down. It suddenly thrust its head against the boy's shoulder and left it there. Francis was too thrilled for words. It was just as if the little horse had said, 'All right. You're my friend. I'll trust you and do what you say!'

The man who had helped to break down the door came to find Francis. 'Hallo, Scout!' he said. 'You did a jolly good deed in rescuing that terrified little creature. Is he all right now?'

'I think so,' said Francis. 'What is to happen to him?'

'Goodness knows!' said the man. 'All the sheds are gone now – even the one the pony was in. We've saved the shop and the rooms over it, though. Bad luck for poor old Miller.'

'Yes. Terribly bad luck,' said Francis. 'But what about the pony? I'm afraid he'll bolt if I leave him.'

'Where can he go, now?' wondered the man. 'He ought to be stabled for the night – but it's so late.'

A brilliant idea suddenly flashed into Francis's mind. The old stables at Green Meadows! Of course, of course, of course! He could take this little pony there!

'I think I know what to do,' he told the man. 'I come from Green Meadows – that big old house, you know, not far from the new block of flats. Well, we've got some old stables there. I could take him there for the night.'

'Good idea!' said the man. 'That will be one good thing

done. I'll tell the police you're doing that – they've been asking about the pony. They can come and see you about him tomorrow morning.'

So by the light of a rather small moon, Francis led the little pony back to Green Meadows. It went with him willingly. It liked this boy and trusted him. Its little hooves clip-clopped along the road, and in at the back gate, and up to the stables.

'In you go, Flash,' said Francis. 'That's right. What a good little thing you are! Now, just stand there while I tie you to the post. Can't have you wandering about, you know. I'll get you some straw to lie on. And would you like some water to drink?'

Flash would! Flash was very thirsty indeed, and drank a lot of water from the bucket Francis brought. The boy couldn't think what to give him to eat, but he remembered the apples up in the stable loft – getting rather soft and uneatable now, for it was April. Still, Flash didn't seem to mind at all. He munched four apples with pleasure, and gave little 'hrrrrrrumphs' of thanks. He wasn't really hungry – but the apples were an unexpected treat in the middle of the night.

It was cold in the stables, because the doors were always left open. Francis fetched an old rug and threw it over the pony. 'There!' he said. 'You can stand up and sleep or lie down and sleep just as you like. I don't know enough about horses to know which you do! Goodnight, Flash – sleep well, and don't feel afraid any more!'

He shut the stable doors and went creeping back to the house. Nobody had awakened, nobody at all! Francis was just taking off his clothes when he heard a loud whinny from the distant stables.

It was Flash. He didn't like being alone. He had remembered the flames and the noise and the heat. He felt lonely and strange in these stables. He wanted that boy.

'Well! I can't have him whinnying all night and waking everyone up,' thought Francis. 'I'd better spend the night in the stables. But I'll want a good supply of rugs – and my old eiderdown.'

He had taken off his uniform. He pulled on some shorts, two jerseys, and put his long thick dressing gown over the top. He pulled his eiderdown off his bed and then got two rugs from the hall cupboard. Surely he would be warm enough now!

Rex heard him creeping down the path and began to bark from his kennel. Goodness! Now *he* would wake everyone up! Francis stole down to the dog.

'Be quiet, you silly! It's only me. Do you want to come with me? All right – but don't frighten Flash!'

He lifted the dog over the wire netting and Rex padded happily at his heels. What an adventure! Where was Francis going with all those rugs?

They came to the stables. Flash was lying down in the straw, wide awake. He gave a little whinny when he heard Francis and smelt him.

Francis made himself a pile of straw beside Flash and burrowed into it, on top of a rug. He wrapped himself up in the eiderdown, and pulled the second rug on top of him. Rex flopped down on his legs, and made a nice warm spot there. Flash made another on his left side! In fact, Flash was so very warm that Francis soon threw off the rug.

The pony was happy and at peace. That boy was here with him. He was safe. There was a dog too, but if he was the boy's friend, well, that was all right.

They all three slept peacefully through the rest of the night. The sun came up, and they still slept. Mother got up early as she always did, and soon Sam awoke too. He sat up and yawned.

Then he noticed that Francis's bed was empty. His dressing gown was gone. His eiderdown too! Whatever had happened in the night? He rushed to his mother.

'Mother! Where's Francis? He's gone! His bed is empty!' And then, dear me, what a search began! 'Francis! Francis! Where are you!'

Granny was dressing, and she heard the cries. She slipped on a dressing gown and joined the hunt. Daddy was still in bed, for he didn't get up till after breakfast, when Mother had time to help him to dress. He lay and listened, feeling worried.

What a search there was for Francis! Mother began to feel more and more upset. It wasn't like Francis to slip off like this – in his dressing gown too! And why were his pyjamas still on his bed – crumpled, showing that he must have slept in them?

'He may be with Rex,' suddenly said Clare. 'He might have heard him barking in the night and gone to see him. I'll run down to the kennel and look.'

So down she went – but in half a minute she was back.

'Mother, Rex isn't there either! What *can* have happened?'

Sam went to the kitchen door and called loudly. 'Rex! Rex!'

Rex was lying against the sleeping Francis in the stables. The door was shut, and the stables were a little distance away, but Rex's sharp ears hear Sam's shout. He got up quietly and ran to the stable door. It was old and did not shut properly. Rex pawed at it and it opened a little. He squeezed through and ran to the house.

'Mother! Here's Rex!' called Sam. 'Rex, where is Francis? Tell us!'

'Woof!' said Rex, and turned round and trotted off, looking round as if to say, 'Come on! Follow me! I'll take you to him.'

'He knows!' said Clare. 'Mother, let's follow him.'

'Oh dear – I do hope he isn't lying hurt anywhere!' said Mother anxiously, hurrying after Rex, followed by Granny. Clare and Sam ran in front, excited.

'He's taking us to the stables!' said Sam. 'We never thought of going there to look!'

They came to the stables. Rex pushed at the door and it swung open. He went in, his tail wagging. Everyone followed. What a sight they saw!

There was Francis, curled up in his eiderdown fast asleep on the straw beside a small chestnut pony! Flash looked round as if to say, 'I'm sorry – but I can't get up because I don't want to wake this boy!'

'Francis!' shouted Sam in amazement, and Francis woke up with a jump! How comfortable he was! How warm! He thought he was in bed. He opened his eyes and stretched.

'Francis, dear!' said Mother's voice, anxiously. Francis sat up at once. He looked round in astonishment. Where was he? And then, as Flash the pony struggled to get to his feet he remembered everything! The fire! The burning shed, the pony, bringing him here – yes, of course. Goodness, whatever time was it?

'Am I late for school?' he said, and tried to get up. But the eiderdown was round him and he rolled over. Sam gave a squeal of laughter and ran to help.

'Francis, *do* tell us the meaning of this,' said Granny, her voice sharp with bewilderment. 'You out here – with a pony! Where did he come from?'

'Oh dear – I meant to get up early and get back to the house and tell you all,' said Francis, standing up at last in his crumpled dressing gown. 'Mother, it's all right. I'll tell you everything.'

'Come indoors then,' said Mother. 'Good gracious! Whatever will you do next? Hiding dogs – and now a pony! Come indoors, dear.'

They all went up into Daddy's bedroom, because he was almost beside himself wanting to know what was happening, but he couldn't get out of bed without help. Rex trotted in too, and behind him came Dapple the kitten. Mr Black was already there, lying majestically on Daddy's bed.

'Daddy! Francis has got a pony in the stables!' cried Sam. 'A pony!'

Francis began to tell his story. Everyone listened

breathlessly – what a tale! Sam's eyes grew wide when he heard about the fire. Mother swelled with pride when she heard how her Francis had gone out to help, and had actually broken down a shed door to get out little Flash.

'Well!' said Daddy, when the exciting tale was finished at last. 'I'm proud of you, Francis. I know you're a Scout, and it's your duty to do what you can, where you can, whenever you can – but it takes a *brave* Scout to do what you did! Well done.'

Francis glowed with pleasure. Daddy himself was brave, very brave. He had won many medals, and one of them was for great bravery. Now he had called Francis brave. Sam gave him a slap on the back.

'Good old Francis!' he said.

'But what are you going to do with the pony?' said Granny.

'The police will be coming about it,' said Francis. 'They'll know what to do. Oh dear – I wish it was Saturday! Mother, it's getting late, isn't it? Goodness, look at the time! We'll be late for school!'

'Now don't get into a state,' said Granny. 'I'll brush Rex and give him fresh water, and I'll see to the kitten, and I'll slip along and see to the pony too. Well – it's good to see a pony in the old stables once more.'

'You know all about horses, don't you, Granny?' said Sam. 'You know better than Francis does. Have *you* ever slept beside a horse all night?'

'Once. When I was as small as you,' said Granny. 'I'll tell you about that another time. You don't get me telling you stories now, just as we've all got to rush and hurry.'

Francis only just had time after breakfast to go and give the pony a pat and a stroke, and whisper a few words in his ear. He would have to run all the way to school as it was. But who cared? He had had an adventure – and now there was a pony in the stables. How Francis hoped he would be there when he got back!

'I'll get that pony out into the orchard,' said Granny after breakfast. 'It's a beautiful day, and he can crop the grass there.'

She looked excited and happy. She didn't say one cross word to Daddy. And, dear me, she didn't even stop to help Mother wash up! Mother was most amused.

'The old lady's happy,' said Daddy smiling. 'How she must have missed all the animals she used to be surrounded with – her dogs, cats, horses, pigeons! Now she only has Mr Black, and the wild birds she feeds – and a borrowed kitten and dog!'

'She's a real animal-lover,' said Mother. 'She always has been. She taught me to be too, though since I've been so busy I haven't more than a minute a day to think of birds and animals!'

'No. You think of your family all the time, and you have to give up all the things you used to love to do,' said Daddy, reaching out for Mother's hand as she passed. 'You don't read any more, you don't go walking in the woods and hills – you don't have any time to spend on yourself!'

'But I'm happy!' said Mother, giving Daddy a kiss at the back of his neck. He always liked that. 'I've got you and the children and Granny – and we're a *proper* family, aren't we? All for one and one for all!'

She ran out into the kitchen to go on with her work. Daddy picked up the paper but he didn't read it. If only, only, only he could get well again! When would Dr Miles come and see him – was it tomorrow? Perhaps he had heard of some new treatment; perhaps one day he would get out of this wheelchair and walk about and teach the boys cricket, and take Clare for walks, and see that Mother didn't do so much! Perhaps! Always perhaps!

Granny bustled in, all her chains jingling merrily. 'That's a fine little pony!' she said. 'Pretty too. He reminds me of one I had when I was Clare's age. The gallops I had on him! I've given him a grooming and now I've turned him out into the orchard. He's as happy as a sandboy!'

Daddy looked out of the window. 'My word – it seems strange to see a pony grazing there!' he said. 'What a dear little fellow! He must have been scared last night, when the fire broke out.'

'Yes. He's got a hurt leg,' said Granny. 'He must have hurt it when he galloped round the shed in fright. I've dealt with it as best I can. It's nothing much. Now I must go and help in the kitchen. Dear dear – my poor daughter will think I have deserted her!'

Daddy stared after Granny. She seemed quite different! He looked at the little pony grazing happily under the trees, with Rex running there too, pleased at having a new four-legged companion.

The kitten jumped up on Daddy's lap and he stroked it. It patted his hand with a soft paw, curled up into a ball with its tail wrapped round it, and fell asleep. Mr Black watched from a nearby chair, and then calmly jumped down, walked to Daddy, and climbed slowly up on him. Mr Black was always careful of Daddy's legs! He settled himself down on top of Dapple, who squeezed himself out, half-suffocated. Daddy laughed. What a pair!

The police didn't come that morning. In fact, they didn't come at all. But just as the family had finished their midday meal, a young man came wandering up the path to find the back door.

'Oh dear – I'm afraid he's come to take Flash away,' said Clare, mournfully. 'I feel it in my bones. Oh, it was so nice rushing home from school and finding Flash in the orchard. I wish we could have a ride on him before he goes. He's just the size for us!'

'He whinnied like anything when I went to him,' said Francis. 'He rubbed his head against me. Granny, you were very very lucky to have a pony of your own when you were small.

'Yes, I was,' said Granny. 'I'd have liked my grandchildren to have had ponies too. But things change so. I had too much – they have too little.'

'We haven't,' said Sam, sturdily. 'I like my home. I like everyone here. I don't want anything changed.'

'Yes, you do. You said you wanted to sleep in *my* bed, because yours was lumpy,' said Francis. 'You wanted to change over!'

'I don't mean things like that,' said Sam. 'I mean . . .'

But what Sam meant nobody heard, because it was at that very moment that the young man walked up to the kitchen door. He rapped loudly with his knuckles.

Everyone but Daddy rushed into the kitchen, certain that the young man had come for Flash. Well, Flash wasn't going without a lot of goodbyes said to him.

'Good afternoon,' said the young man. 'Er – I've come about my uncle's pony. I heard you had him here. Can I have a word with you, please, Mrs Marshall?'

'Come in,' said Mother, and he stepped in. The three children looked at him. What was he going to say?

The young man was very polite. He took off his cap as soon as he got indoors, and didn't sit down till he was asked to. He twisted his cap round and round in his big hands and looked very worried.

'I'm so sorry that your uncle's sheds were all burnt down last night,' said Mother, kindly. 'I hear that your uncle was taken to hospital yesterday, very ill. What bad luck to happen all at once!'

'Yes, it is,' said the young man. 'I'm very worried. My uncle's too ill for me to tell him about all this – there's no one to take on his business, because his wife, my aunt, is too upset to leave him. So I've got to decide everything myself.'

'Can we help you?' said Daddy. 'What's your biggest worry?'

'Well, you see, I and my brother run a greengrocer's business in the next town,' said the young man. 'My name's Miller, like my uncle's – Sid Miller – and it was my uncle who set us up in business. He was good to us, very good. And now I've got to make up my mind whether to sell his business or close it down, in case he doesn't get better – or whether to hope for the best and come over here myself and run it, hoping he *will* get better and be strong enough to run it himself. My brother could run our own business by himself for a bit.'

'I see,' said Daddy. 'It's a big decision for you to make. But I should certainly take on your uncle's business for the time being, if your brother can manage on his own. It would be a terrible blow to your uncle to come out of hospital and find his business sold! What does your aunt say?'

'She says I'm to do what I think best,' said Sid. 'But she's so upset about everything that I can't really get a word of sense out of her, poor thing.'

'What do you want to do about the pony?' said Granny, and her chains jingled as she leaned forward.

'That's what I came about, of course,' said Sid. 'Not to worry you with my troubles! I just told you those to explain things a bit. Now, suppose I do what Mr Marshall here says – leave my brother to run our business, and come over here to run my uncle's – I can't use the pony.'

'Why not?' asked Daddy.

'For two reasons,' said Sid, earnestly. 'One is that the delivery cart is burnt; and the other is that I'm used to taking things out in a delivery van. Uncle was a bit old-fashioned – he didn't hold with delivery vans; so he took out the pony and wagon, and went round selling vegetables and fruit, and delivering them too. Of course, he had his delivery boys on bicycles, as well.'

'I see,' said Daddy. 'Well, go on.'

'Well – if I'm not using the pony I ought to sell him,' said Sid. 'He would fetch in a bit of money to help pay for things; my uncle wasn't insured for the sheds. But the thing is – old Uncle Fred was so *fond* of that pony I believe it would break his heart if he found him gone when he got out of hospital.'

There was a silence. Then Daddy spoke again. 'We can't buy him, if that's what you're after,' he said. 'We've no money ourselves.'

'No. I wasn't going to ask you that,' said Sid. 'I'm fond of my uncle, and I'd like to keep the little old pony for him, if he comes back. But where can I keep him? They charge a lot up at the Riding Stables. What I came to ask was this – and please don't take offence, sir – I've heard you're all fond of animals – and – well, couldyoulookaftertheponyhereforme?'

The last nine words came out in such a rush, and in such a desperate voice, that nobody understood them. Sid repeated them. 'Could you look after the pony for me here? I'd pay you what you ask, because I know you wouldn't charge like a horse stables would.'

Sid's request was so very unexpected that it took everyone by surprise. Then Francis leapt up with a shout:

'He wants us to have Flash! *He wants us to have Flash!* Yes, we will, we will, we will!'

Clare's face glowed. Sam looked solemn and thrilled at the same time, and began to whistle softly.

But Daddy damped it all down. 'No,' he said firmly. 'No. A horse needs quite a lot of looking after. The children are at school all day, and it would fall to my wife to see to the pony. She has too much to do already.'

'Daddy!' cried all three children in dismay. But Daddy was quite firm.

'I said no. And I mean no. I'd like to help Sid, but I'm not adding to your mother's burdens. It's no use you children telling me you can do everything. You can't. I said no, and that's the end of it!'

Clare burst into tears. Sam stamped out of the room, not whistling any more. And then something most unexpected happened. Granny began to speak.

'I agree with every word you've said, John,' she said to Daddy. 'I won't have any more put on to my daughter, and as you say the children will be busy at school. But – we *will* have the pony, because *I* will look after him! I know all about horses, I was brought up here with that stable full of them. *I* will be responsible for Flash, and he shall live in *my* stable, and eat *my* grass in *my* orchard. I say yes. And I *mean* yes!'

The old lady jingled all her chains, and sat up straight, looking so fierce that Daddy burst into laughter. He laughed and laughed. Clare flew to the door and shouted after Sam.

'Sam, Sam! It's all right. Come back at once.' And Sam came in quickly, looking round hopefully at everyone. Whatever was Daddy laughing at?

'All right, all right,' said Daddy at last. 'I'm defeated. I forgot you knew so much about horses, Granny – and as you say, the stables are yours, the orchard, and even the grass in it! And if you'll look after the pony, well, I have nothing more to say. I am quite sure that both you and the pony will be happy!'

Granny beamed round. She had got her way and she always loved that. She turned graciously to Sid. 'That's settled then,' she said. 'We keep the pony. You can supply his corn and let us have hay or straw, I suppose?'

'Oh yes – yes! Anything!' said the relieved Sid. 'And please let the kids ride him – he's used to that. I and my brother rode him twelve years ago, when *we* were kids. He's about fourteen now, and he's gentle and hard-working. I'd have hated to get rid of old Flash.'

Sam began to whistle loudly, and not even Granny stopped him. Sid got up to go, twisting his cap round and round so quickly that it quite fascinated Clare. He cleared his throat as if he were going to make a little speech. Daddy stopped him.

'You don't need to thank us – we're glad to help you. And remember this, Sid – hard work never hurt anyone. So go to it, and do your best!'

'Thank you. I'm not afraid of hard work. Not a bit,' said Sid. 'You've been very nice to me. Er – what shall I pay you for your kindness, sir? Would you prefer money, or shall I bring you fresh vegetables free, each week?'

'Nothing of the sort, young man,' said Granny, sitting up very straight again. 'I'm doing this because I love horses, and it's good to help a young man who's doing a bit of kindness himself – and you're doing your best for your uncle! Don't you dare to mention payment again! My grass is free, and so is my orchard!'

Sid went very red at this outburst, and looked

bewildered. Mother stood up and took him to the door, smiling.

'My mother sounds fiercer than she is,' she said. 'But she's kindness itself.'

'Thank you,' said Sid. 'I'll repay you some day – in spite of what the old lady says, God bless her!'

Sid walked off happily, looking round him at the untidy, neglected garden as he went down the path. Gracious – they must be poor to have a lovely place like this in such an untidy state! Couldn't they even afford a jobbing gardener? Sid saw Flash grazing happily in the orchard, and went to him.

'You're in clover, old fellow!' he said. 'Enjoy your holiday! That's what it will be for you, till we get things fixed up. And you deserve it, you're such a hard-working little chap!'

Flash knew Sid and he put his head on the young man's shoulder. It was a little way he had. He didn't quite understand what was happening – but he certainly was enjoying himself!

There was enormous excitement as soon as Sid had gone. Sam flung himself on Granny and almost knocked her off her chair. 'You're good, good, good!' he said. 'I always knew you were, but now I think you're even gooder!'

Clare sat with her eyes shining. A pony in the orchard every day. *Almost* their own. One they could ride!

Francis rubbed his hands in delight. The stables! He would clean out one of the stalls and make it beautiful for Flash. He would look in the harness room and see if there was an old saddle there – and a bridle. Granny would show him how to put them on Flash. He would polish the leather till it shone!

Granny got up, jingling loudly. She felt very proud of herself. 'Well, that's that,' she said. 'Sam, stop hugging me so hard round the waist, you're squeezing my dinner! And remember, please, *I've* undertaken to look after the pony. You children can just play with him when you've time, and ride him – but I'll do all the work for him. I don't mind you helping at weekends.'

'I'm going to help all day long,' said Sam, solemnly. 'All – day – long!'

'You're not,' said Mother. 'You're going to school. Don't be silly.'

'I'm not going to school,' said Sam, and he gave a sudden squeal of laughter. 'It's holidays next week – four weeks! Ha ha, Mother – you forgot!'

'Golly – so it is,' said Clare. 'Oh, Granny – we *can* help then! Holidays, holidays, holidays – they're coming at *exactly* the right time!'

'Look at the clock!' said Mother, suddenly. 'Off to school, all of you. Wait, wait! Brush your hair, please, and . . .'

But the children didn't wait to listen. They knew all that by heart. 'Brush your hair, wash your hands, tidy yourself, please!' sang Clare, light-heartedly. And in two minutes' time they all three rushed helter-skelter down the path. How happy they were!

7

Easter Holidays

Flash was a great success. Granny loved him with all her heart, and spent a lot of time with him. She still helped Mother as much as ever, but she gave up her afternoon rest so that she would have plenty of time for any jobs for the pony.

At first Mother was cross when she found that the old lady was no longer resting in the afternoon – but Daddy stopped her scolding Granny.

'Don't prevent the old lady from going out and seeing to the pony,' said Daddy. 'All this fresh air and exercise and being happy with Flash is doing her a world of good. She isn't nearly so crotchety now that she has something else to think of beside the house and the family!'

'You're right, as usual,' said Mother. '*You* like going down in your wheelchair to the orchard too, and being with Flash and Rex, don't you? You and Granny are a pair! It's a lovely place now, down there under the pear blossom, with daffodils all round your feet.'

'And the cuckoo playing hide-and-seek and calling cuckoo all the time!' said Daddy. 'I wish you'd more time to get down there with us, dear – it's so lovely now. Leave the jobs and spend some time out in the sun!'

'I can't,' said Mother. 'One day, perhaps. The children will be home all day for the holidays soon, and you know what a lot more work that means – though I love doing it for them.'

When the holidays came the three children were as happy as the day was long. They persuaded Mother to let them have their meals in the garden, and Francis carried all the trays out himself. It certainly was lovely out there in the April sunshine – and, as Daddy said, it was one way of getting Mother out-of-doors!

Granny was very, very busy at the beginning of those holidays. She and the children cleared out everything in the harness room, and a saddle was found to fit Flash, and a bridle too. The stirrup straps were broken and had to be mended. They cleaned and polished all the leather till Clare could almost see her face in the saddle.

They cleaned out one of the stalls in the stable, and put hay in the manger, though Flash much preferred the fresh grass in the orchard. It was long and lush and brilliant green. The children couldn't wait for the saddle and bridle to be ready. They rode him bareback!

He was a solid little pony, good-tempered and cheerful, though a bit on the fat side. When Sam rode him his short legs stuck out comically over Flash's fat flanks, and he found it very difficult to keep on. He rolled off plenty of times, but as Sam was as plump as the pony, he didn't mind in the least.

'I fall on the place where I'm fattest,' he told Granny. 'So it doesn't hurt, it just takes my breath away. Why don't *you* have a ride, Granny? You're little. You wouldn't be too heavy.'

'If you think that an old lady like me is going to gallop bareback under the pear trees, you're mistaken,' said Granny. 'Go on with you! I never know whether you mean things or not.'

'Oh, I *do*,' said Sam surprised. 'I thought you *would* like to ride Flash just for once. Perhaps you ride him when we're not looking?'

'Sam! Don't be absurd,' said Granny, and gave him a tap on his arm. 'Go and get some clean straw for me, please. Sid brought a whole lot up yesterday.'

Sid was quite a friend, almost at once. He brought up straw and hay and oats and carrots for Flash. He made friends with all the children and with Rex and Dapple the kitten.

'You've got a lovely place here,' he said one evening, looking round. 'But it's so neglected. It gets on my nerves when I look round and see all those weeds and tangled grass and the mess everywhere.'

'We haven't time to garden as well as everything else,' said Francis. 'We just keep a bit in front of the house weeded and planted for Mother, and that's all. We've had to let the rest go. Mother tried to do it, but Daddy made her stop, she got so tired.'

Sid sat silent for a moment and then spoke, rather awkwardly. 'Er – I've got a bit of time this evening,' he said. 'I suppose you wouldn't let me mess about in the garden a bit? I love gardening, I was going to *be* a gardener, but my uncle wanted me to set up in the greengrocery business.'

'Do what you like,' said Francis. 'There are tools in the stables. Hey, Dan – show Sid where the tools are, will you?'

Dan was up at Green Meadows almost every evening, partly to be with Rex and partly because he enjoyed playing – and working – with Francis and the other two. He copied Francis in everything, and admired him very much. He was determined to be a Scout. He had been very much impressed at the Scout meetings he had attended. The things they did! Gracious! – it was a real boy's job that – being a Scout.

He did good deeds in secret, pretending that he was a Scout already. So he was always ready to give a hand to anyone, especially the Marshall family. He went off at once with Sid and showed him the tools.

'Why don't you come and help me do a spot of work down in that garden?' said Sid, suddenly. 'You're a big strong lad – I reckon you and I together could make part of the garden very nice for Mrs Marshall.'

'All right,' said Dan, surprised. 'But – are you going to come another time then?'

'Yes. I've been worrying about how to pay back for the old lady's kindness about Flash,' said Sid. 'And it suddenly came to me this evening. "Silly fool!" I said to myself. "Look at this garden staring you in the face! Get down to it, Sid," I said. "That's the way to pay back the Marshalls' kindness!"'

Dan agreed. 'I'll help too,' he said. 'You see, they won't let me pay money or buy them sweets, so my mum comes each Wednesday and helps in the house – for nothing, of course. But I don't do anything, so I'll do this. It would be a good deed, wouldn't it?'

'You a Scout then?' said Sid. 'No? Well, you don't need to be a Scout to do good deeds. Come on. You take the spade, I'll take the fork, the barrow, and the trowel.'

Mother was amazed when she came down the garden to get some mint for mint sauce. There was Sid digging hard in a piece of ground full of overgrown rose trees – and there was Dan busy grubbing up weeds, and trying to find the edges of the bed!

'What in the world are you doing?' said Mother, astonished.

Sam was there, waiting to wheel the barrow to the rubbish heap when it was full. 'They're paying back,' he said. 'Don't tell them to stop, Mother. They're not paying *you* back – they're paying Granny. She came up and said they could. Aren't you, Sid and Dan?'

Sid looked sheepish, and stood up straight, his face red and hot with hard work. He was enjoying himself.

'I like this kind of thing,' he said. 'I wanted to be a gardener once. I'd like to get a bit of this garden nice for you all. It's a shame to let it go like this.'

Mother was touched. 'That's good of you,' she said, and went indoors smiling, to tell the news to Daddy. She took the mint with her, sniffing its clean strong smell.

'Good for Sid!' said Daddy. 'He's not afraid of work, that young man. He'll go far. It's the lazy ones who stay put and never get anywhere. I like Sid.'

Francis was very happy. He had Rex, he had the mad, bad little kitten, and now he had Flash. There was only one thing that worried him – and it worried Granny too.

It was Flash's hurt leg. The wound on it had seemed to heal all right – but now it had broken out again and Flash had begun to limp. Granny had done all she could, but she was afraid the leg was poisoned. She and Francis discussed the matter together.

'There's a vet at Langham Down, six miles away,' said Granny. 'But Flash couldn't walk all that way to him with his hurt leg, and we couldn't afford to ask the vet to come here and see to him. He might have to do quite a lot to Flash's leg.'

'I've saved up some money,' said Francis.

'It would need a lot, I'm afraid,' said Granny, 'if Flash has to have treatment. We can't ask Sid for the money – he's running his uncle's business at a loss, as it is, till he gets used to it. He's only a young fellow, and hasn't any money saved up that he can draw on. This is a thing we must settle ourselves, Francis.'

'The leg looks a *bit* better tonight,' said Francis, looking at the sore place. Granny didn't think so. What *could* they do? Money, money, money – she had been spending too much lately, and she had hardly any left till her next quarter's cheque came along.

It was Rita who solved the whole problem. She came to be with Dapple, and to bring him a new rubber ball to play with. She saw Granny and ran up to her with Dapple.

'Isn't the kitten growing?' she said. 'Doesn't he look well?'

'He does – and you're looking a lot better yourself!'

said Granny. 'Playing up here in the open air is better for you than being mewed up in a flat with no garden to give you space to play in the sunshine! Look here a minute – we are worried about Flash's leg. It seems bad, doesn't it?'

Rita looked. She knew nothing about horses except that Flash was lovely to ride, but even she could see that the leg was bad, and that poor little Flash was in pain.

'Why don't you take him to the Animal Van?' she said, rubbing Flash's long velvety nose gently. She loved him as much as the others did. 'It's in Packhorse Dene today, but it will be gone tomorrow. It's on its way to Langham Down.'

'Whatever's the Animal Van?' said Francis in astonishment. 'I've never heard of it!'

'Well, I don't know much about it,' said Rita, playing with the kitten. 'I only heard someone telling my mother that she once had a sick cat, and took it to the Animal Van and the Animal Doctor inside cured it. So I thought he might cure Flash's leg.'

'What *can* she mean?' wondered Granny, as Rita darted after the kitten, which had scampered under a bush.

'I'll ask Sid. Maybe he knows. Sid! Come here a minute. Do you know anything about an Animal Van with an Animal Doctor inside – or is it just something Rita's made up?'

'The Animal Van? Oh, yes – that's one of the motor-caravans belonging to the P.D.S.A.,' said Sid. 'I once took my dog there.'

'P.D.S.A.! And what does *that* stand for?' said Granny.

'People's Dispensary for Sick Animals,' said Sid promptly. 'It's a society that is run for sick animals. They have vans out all over the country – Caravan Dispensaries is their right name, but the kids call them Animal Vans. Anyone can take a sick or hurt animal to the Van Doctor, and get it seen to.'

'Van Doctor! I've never heard of anyone called that before!' said Granny.

'Oh well – the right name is Technical Officer – T.O.s they are called for short,' said Sid. 'But most Technical Officers are known as Animal Doctors by the children. It's quite a thrill when the Animal Van comes along with the Animal Doctor inside, ready to help.'

'Do they charge much?' asked Granny.

'They don't charge a penny!' said Sid. 'Not a penny! The help is for the people who can't afford to pay fees, you see. It's all run and paid for by animal lovers who can't bear animals to be sick or hurt and not have help. So the Animal Doctors never charge anything. Honest! Of course – if you like to give what you can afford, they're jolly pleased. There's always a collecting box there, just in case! Why do you want to know about it?'

'Well, look at Flash's leg,' said Granny. 'I thought it was better – but it's broken out again. Could we take him to the Animal Van, do you think – or Caravan Dispensary as you said it was called?'

'My word – it's bad, isn't it?' said Sid, alarmed. 'The van's at Packhorse Dene this evening: it may be gone after that. Can't we take old Flash now, straight away, before he gets too bad to walk? Poor old fellow, he's in pain.'

'We'll take him,' said Granny, in her most determined voice. 'He can walk that far, though I'd really rather he didn't. But if we wait and send a message to the Caravan Dispensary, it might just have left. Come along, Flash, dear old boy.'

So, attended by Granny, Sid, Dan, Rita, and the three Marshall children, Flash set off slowly. It was quite a procession that moved off down the lane towards Packhorse Dene. In her anxiety to get to the van before it was too late, Granny quite forgot to tell Mother. So Mother was amazed when she came out into the garden, to find it completely deserted. No Granny, no Sid, no children, no pony, dog, or kitten. How very extraordinary!

Flash limped along slowly. He was such a good, patient little thing that Clare felt as if she would burst into tears.

'I wish I could carry him!' she said. 'He must wonder why we're taking him for a walk just when his leg is hurting him most. I don't think we ought to!'

'It's all right, darling,' said Granny. 'It isn't very far. He knows we're all sorry for him.'

Rex ran ahead, delighted at this unexpected walk on a lovely April evening. Celandines shone in the ditches and white violets made the evening air smell sweet. It was a beautiful walk to Packhorse Dene – if only Flash had been able to walk properly too!

They came into the quaint little village. The van was still there. The Animal Doctor's sister ran the little inn at the corner near by, and he had been given permission to see his sister and spend the night there. The van was open – and anyone could bring sick animals or birds to be examined.

The news had gone round that the caravan was spending the night at the village. 'The Dispensary is here with its T.O.!' said the grown-ups. 'That Animal Van is here with the Animal Doctor!' said the children. So when Flash and his companions walked into the village street, they saw quite a little crowd of people waiting near a big cream caravan with the letters P.D.S.A. in blue lettering along the sides.

A small man with a firm, kindly face was standing at the doorway, handing a cat to a small girl. He twinkled at her through his glasses.

'Here you are. Here's your Tibs. Nothing much wrong. I've dosed her and she'll be quite all right in a day or two.'

'Oh, thank you!' said the small girl, and clutched Tibs eagerly. 'Thank you! Oh, Tibs, do you feel better?'

She went off happily. The Animal Doctor looked round at the waiting people. 'Who's next? You with the dog?'

A boy got up with a small dog in his arms. The dog lay still and seemed in pain.

'I've brought my dog, sir,' said the boy. 'He got into a fight. His neck's badly bitten. Oh, sir, he won't die, will he? He's such a *good* dog!'

'Dear me, no! I'll soon see to him,' said the doctor, glancing at the wound. 'Come along into the van with me. He'll feel better with you there. You can help me. We'll clean out the wound, and I'll give you ointment to put on it. It's a good thing it's at the back of his neck. He can't lick himself there!'

The boy went into the van and the door closed. Everyone hoped and hoped that the dog would be all right. In a surprisingly short time the door opened again, and out came the boy with his dog, beaming all over his face.

'I held him while the doctor did his neck,' he announced proudly. 'Wags was as good as gold. You'll soon be all right now, won't you, old boy? I've got your ointment in my pocket, and I'm going to carry you all the way home!'

There was another cat to be seen too, with a swollen face, and a canary in a cage, that had hurt its wing. There was even a mouse with a broken tail!

The child with the cat went into the van to hold her pet while the doctor examined it. She came out very quickly, with the cat still in her arms, looking very sleepy.

'He pulled one of Fluffy's teeth out,' said the little girl. 'It was very, very bad. Now Fluffy's face will be all right. It won't be swollen tomorrow, he says. He just put her to sleep for a minute, and pulled it out then. Fluff never even knew. He's *clever*.'

Soon it was Flash's turn. 'I'll see him where he stands,' said the little Animal Doctor. 'Ah – it's his leg, I see. How did it happen?'

Francis told him. The doctor looked at him. 'Aren't you the boy that rescued a pony from a burning shed?' he said. 'I heard about that. My sister at the inn there told me. Well done!'

He turned to the pony, and rubbed his nose and spoke to him gently before he even examined the leg. Flash pricked up his ears. He liked this man's voice very much. He suddenly put his head on the doctor's shoulder – and then Francis knew that it wouldn't matter what the man did to him, Flash would bear it!

'I'd better take him into my sister's stable, over there at the inn,' said the little doctor. 'I can see to his leg more easily there, in private. I'll just fetch a few things that I shall need from the van.'

Flash was taken across to the inn stable. 'I think I'll have him alone, without anyone with him,' said the man. He shut the door and left everyone outside. Nobody spoke a word. There was complete silence except for a sudden little whinny from Flash, inside the stable.

Clare was in tears. Poor Flash! She put up a sudden little prayer in the way she often did when she was anxious or worried. 'Dear God, please help Flash, please help him, he's so sweet, and you can see how bad his leg is.'

Sam saw Clare's lips moving and he knew what she was doing. He shut his eyes tight and said urgently, 'Please God, look after little Flash, do look after him.'

He opened his eyes – and at the same moment the stable door opened too, and out came Flash with the Doctor, rather bewildered but not at all upset.

'Here he is,' said the little man, smiling. 'Good thing you brought him when you did! The leg was very nasty. But the wound is quite clean now, and I've bandaged his leg well.'

Sid, Francis and Granny all surged forward to take Flash. He still limped, but he seemed quite cheerful.

'Thank you very much,' said Granny. 'I must pay you.'

'We never charge anything,' said the little doctor. 'Not a penny.'

Francis had seen a collection box on the table inside the van. 'I've got some money here,' he said. 'It was lucky I saved it up. I shall put it all into your box!'

Granny put in something too – and then Sid put in a small coin; it was all he could spare.

'I've got a penny,' said Clare, and that went into the collecting box too! The Animal Doctor looked very pleased.

'I've got nothing,' said Sam, mournfully. 'What can I do?'

'Well, why don't you belong to the Busy Bees?' said the little doctor. 'They are children who love animals and care for them and help us in our work. Here – take this form, it tells you all about it. Next time I see you, young man, I hope I shall find you wearing our little yellow badge with the bee on it!'

Sam was delighted. He took the piece of paper, folded it up carefully and put it into his pocket. A Busy Bee! It sounded good. Sam liked to be busy, and he liked bees – nice, humming, buzzing things that made him honey for his tea. Yes, certainly Sam would be a Busy Bee and help this kind man to carry on with his work for animals like Flash and Dapple and Rex!

'Can I have one of those papers too, please,' said Rita, shyly. 'I've got a kitten, look, and I'm an animal lover too. What do Busy Bees do?'

'Ah, you just join and see!' said the man. 'There are plenty of things, and all of them are interesting. Here, take half a dozen forms, your friends may like to see them.'

Rita proudly took the little bundle of papers. She was thrilled to think she had been bold enough to speak out like that, and get the papers. She hugged Dapple and went off, crimson with pleasure.

'Anyone else?' said the little doctor, looking round. There was only one more person who had arrived just after the children, on a bicycle. It was a man with a puppy. He had it in his bicycle basket, a tiny creature that whined feebly.

'Have you got time to see this pup?' asked the man. 'There's something the matter with his leg. It's broken, I think. If you want to shut up for the night I'll bring him in tomorrow, to Langham Down. I can cycle in.'

'Good gracious no! Of course I'll see to him now,' said the doctor. 'Let's have a look at him.'

The man took the puppy from the basket. One leg hung limp and useless. 'Gently, now, gently,' said the Animal Doctor. 'Don't handle him too roughly. Is he yours?'

'No. He belongs to my little girl,' said the man. He

was a rough-looking fellow, with a dirty white scarf round his neck, and hair much too long. 'I've no patience with animals – but she loves this pup, and she's crying her eyes out about him.'

'How did it happen?' said the doctor, stroking the tiny creature gently.

'Well – he got under my feet, and I sent him flying,' said the man. 'Always getting in my way, he is. But then I've no patience with animals in the house.'

'So you kicked him and broke his leg,' said the little man, coldly. 'I see. Well, let us hope that *you* never get into anyone's way, and have your leg broken! Come into the van. I want you to watch what I do – then perhaps you won't kick him again.'

The van door shut. Clare turned to Granny, tears in her eyes. 'I hate that man, I hate him, I hate him, I hate him! I'd like to steal that little puppy and take it to Green Meadows. Horrible, horrible man!'

Sam was white. It had never even occurred to him that anyone could be cruel to animals. He looked very solemn and slipped his arm through Granny's.

'I'm going to be a Busy Bee,' he said. 'Granny, you'll explain about it to me, won't you? I want to get busy immediately, at once, forever!'

'You shall, you shall,' said Granny. 'Now cheer up – look at Flash, he seems better already! Off we go home; and dear oh dear, good gracious me, not one of us remembered to send word in to Mother and Daddy that we were going off to Packhorse Dene with Flash!'

It was late when they got back. Sid left them and went

to the shop, and Rita and Dan slipped off too. Mother, looking out of the gate, suddenly saw her three coming along with Granny and Flash. Rex ran by Francis, and Clare carried Dapple. Where in the world had they been?

'Mother, we've been to the Animal Van!' cried Sam, running to her. 'The S.A.D.P., you know. No, I mean the P.A.S.D. No, I don't mean that either. Clare, what *do* I mean?'

'You mean the P.D.S.A., silly,' said Clare, and out came the whole story to Mother, all about Flash's leg, and the Animal Doctor, and the animals there, and how he had bandaged Flash's leg – dear me, Mother could hardly believe it!

'Now really, you *must* come in to supper,' she said. 'You are a whole hour late! But I don't mind now I know what you've been up to. Naughty Granny, not to send word to me! Granny, you're as bad as the children!'

'Yes, I know,' said Granny, looking quite ashamed of herself. 'I can't think what came over me to forget to tell you. Still, all's well that ends well – and our Flash is soon going to be much better!'

8

Granny's Secret

Early next morning Francis went out to see Flash. He came back at a run. 'Granny! Mother! Flash isn't limping nearly so much this morning! Isn't that good!'

'Splendid,' said Mother.

'He's wandering round the orchard quite happily – and once he forgot to limp!' said Francis. 'Mother, do you know what I'm going to be when I'm grown up?'

'Let me see now – is it a lorry driver, a cowboy or an express train driver?' said Mother. 'I've forgotten!'

'No. I've grown out of those ideas,' said Francis. 'I'm going to be an Animal Doctor and have a caravan of my own, and go round the country helping people with sick animals. Mother, don't you think that's a good idea?'

'Anything that helps others is a grand idea,' said Mother. 'Now, do you mind cleaning the shoes, Francis? You'll not be in time for breakfast if you don't get on with your jobs!'

'Oh dear – life is so exciting these days that there's hardly time to fit in all I've got to do!' said Francis, rushing to get the boot-cleaning box. 'But I like lots of things to be going on, don't you, Mother?'

Mother didn't answer. What she would *really* have

liked was a nice bit of peace, with nothing to do and nothing going on at all – for a week, at any rate! She went on cooking the breakfast. Thank goodness it was Wednesday, and Mrs Oldham was coming.

'We shall soon be able to ride Flash again,' said Clare, at breakfast. 'Granny says his leg will heal quickly now it's been properly seen to. Mother, I've got an idea.'

'Really? How unusual!' said Francis, at once, and got a glare from his sister.

'Be quiet, Francis, I'm not talking to *you*,' she said. 'Mother, listen. Mother, you're not *listening*!'

'Yes, I am,' said Mother. 'What's your idea?'

'Well – my idea is this,' said Clare. 'And Sam thinks it too. We both think Flash would like to pay back for having his leg mended – so, Mother, when he's better, could we let him give other children rides for a little time?'

'They'd pay,' said Sam. 'They said so. They keep asking for rides, but as he's Sid's pony, we didn't like to say yes.'

'Well, I think you must ask Sid,' said Mother. 'I'm sure he won't mind – but ask him first. I think it's a very good idea indeed, so long as you don't let anyone too heavy ride him, and don't overdo it. Flash would quite enjoy it.'

'Oh, Mother! I'm glad you think it's a good idea,' said Clare, beaming. 'Shall we charge from our gate to the end of the lane and back?'

'Yes,' said Mother, smiling. 'That would be a good ride. But don't let anyone ride Flash who might pull at his mouth too hard, or kick his sides to make him go fast.'

'Of course not!' said Sam. 'If anyone does that I'll push him off the pony – crash thud!'

'I shan't let George ride him,' said Clare. 'He took Rex's bone away and made him growl.'

'And not Janet, either,' said Francis, joining in. 'She's . . .'

'You're telling tales!' said Sam. 'You are, you are! And you won't let *me*!'

'Be quiet, Sam,' said Francis. 'Butting in like that! I was *not* going to tell tales.'

'Who's going to take Daddy more toast?' said Mother, changing the subject. 'You, Sam. Carry the rack upstairs carefully, and don't drop the toast on every step!'

'I only did that last year, when I was young,' said Sam solemnly. 'I don't drop things now. Shall I tell Daddy about the rides?'

'Oh yes – he loves to hear the news,' said Mother, and Sam trotted off. His mind was full of Flash and pony rides and full money-boxes, and Busy Bees; really, how exciting everything was!

The Easter holidays really were very thrilling indeed. For one thing, Flash's leg healed rapidly, and in two days' time he was not limping any more – in fact, he took a little gallop round the orchard, using his legs!

Granny untied the bandage. 'Look there!' she said. 'Healed beautifully! Dear old Flash, you're all right now. I'll just rub some of this stuff on, that the Animal Doctor gave me, and put a bandage on for another day or two.'

When Flash's leg was perfectly all right, the Pony Rides began. The news went like lightning round the village, and the nearby housing estate, where the blocks of flats now had a great many people in them.

Children flocked to Green Meadows with their money, their eyes shining. A ride on a pony! Hardly any of them had ridden anything before, except a horse or other animal on a roundabout. They loved Flash with his big brown eyes and thick mane.

Flash felt very important trotting up and down the lane with a different child on his back each time, and Francis, Clare or Sam running beside him. Sam was sure that the pony knew it was part of his 'paying-back,' and was angry with Dan when he laughed at the idea.

'Well, anyway, he's the kind of pony that would *like* to pay back, isn't he?' said Sam, quite fiercely. 'You just dare to say he isn't, Dan!'

'Oh, I *wouldn't* dare!' said Dan, with a grin. 'I'd be afraid you would knock me down and pummel me all over, Sam! I'd have a black eye and a swollen cheek . . .'

That made Sam laugh. He liked Dan. Dan was a Scout now, and very proud of it. He had been enrolled at the last meeting, and had made his Scout promises very solemnly indeed. At home he had the promises framed like a picture, and they were opposite his bed, so that he could see them every morning.

Sam was very interested in Dan's good deeds. 'Do you really do one every day?' he said. 'What do you do. What did you do today? Do tell me. Francis, never, never will! What did you do today, Dan?'

But Dan wouldn't tell either. He just grinned and gave Sam a friendly poke in the ribs. Sam amused him. He was always so solemn, so much in earnest, so very interested in everyone and everything. Dan thought it must be fun to have brothers and sisters. He had none. Still, he had Rex, and that was something.

The pony rides were not the only exciting thing that happened those holidays. As more people came to the flats and learnt that pets were not allowed, but that they could be cared for at Green Meadows, quite a number came to ask Mother if Francis could look after a rabbit, or a guinea pig, or a puppy.

'You see, we thought we'd be allowed to keep a cage on our little balcony,' said one flat-dweller. 'That's not really keeping it *in* the flat, is it? But no – we're not even allowed to do that. And my little boy does love his rabbit. I daren't give it away. Could you possibly find a place for it somewhere? Ronnie would come here each day and see to it himself.'

So the rabbit came, a big white one called Fluffy. The hutch came too – but it was so terribly small that Sid made a nice new one, big and roomy, with a daytime room, and a sleeping room.

'You oughtn't to house a rabbit in such a small hutch,' Francis said to Ronnie. 'It's unkind. And look, don't give him his food so wet. Goodness, fancy keeping an animal and not even knowing how to feed him properly. Now look here: unless you feed him and look after him the proper way – the way I tell you – I won't have him here.'

'All right,' said Ronnie, meekly. He was a bit older than Sam, very spoilt and cheeky. But he was so anxious about his rabbit that he didn't dare to behave badly at Green Meadows. He caught sight of Francis's new badge. All three children, and Dan and Rita too, had joined the Busy Bees, and now wore the little yellow badges with the bee on. The money that Flash collected went into an empty honey pot, ready to send off to Busy Bees' headquarters – Flash was 'paying-back'!

'We're bees, and we're collecting honey in the honey pot,' said Sam to Ronnie, when Ronnie paid for a ride and put the money into the jar. Ronnie hadn't known what Sam meant, but now he saw Francis's yellow bee-badge, and he asked him about it.

'What's that?' he said.

Francis explained. '*You* ought to belong,' he told Ronnie. 'For two reasons. You love your rabbit, so you're an animal lover, but you don't look after him properly, so you ought to learn how to. You soon know a lot about animals if you're a Busy Bee.'

And a week later Ronnie proudly displayed the little yellow badge too! 'We're quite a hive!' said Mother. 'Let's have a hive of Busy Bees here and call it Green Meadows Hive. We can have meetings and tea-parties, and collect all kinds of honey between us – money to send up to headquarters! And tinfoil and stamps – all kinds of things!'

Not only Ronnie's rabbit came. A guinea pig came next, a dear little fellow with no tail at all. He belonged to a boy called Harry, and Francis never had any need to take him to task for not seeing to Gilbert the guinea pig properly. In fact, Harry was so anxious about him that he used to visit him quite late at night, and make Rex bark frantically when he heard someone stealing quietly up the garden path!

A puppy came, a mad little creature, who made friends with Dapple at once. He was put in Rex's old pen, for Rex now had the free run of the whole place, of course.

The puppy was quite untrained, and Pam and Sue, the twins who owned him, had no idea of how to train him.

'Look here,' said Francis, who was now quite an important person, dealing with so many animals and children, 'look here, Pam and Sue – do you want your dog run over? Because he will be, unless you train him to walk to heel in the road. You must be mad, playing ball with him when you take him into the lane! Sid told me he nearly ran him over when he was out in the delivery van, and passed you this morning.'

'Well, how *do* we train a dog?' said Sue. 'I mean – Pongo is so mad that I don't see how he *can* be trained.'

Francis called to Dan. 'Hey, Dan? Done your good deed for today? Well, here's one for you. Give these kids a lesson on how to train a dog – they're hopeless!'

So Dan took *them* in hand and the puppy too. Really, Green Meadows was a very busy place those holidays!

And then one day a man called at Green Meadows. Mother wasn't about, so he saw Granny. He was shabbily dressed, but neat and clean. He took off his cap when he spoke to Granny.

'Excuse me,' he said. 'I come from one of the new little

houses beyond the blocks of flats. I keep pigeons –
fantails, very pretty they are. And now I've been told that
the rule of the blocks of flats about keeping pets is to
apply to us people in the little houses too. And I heard
that you took in creatures here. I wondered if you took
birds?'

Granny looked round cautiously. She wasn't at all sure
that Mother would welcome pigeons. She had already
said that there were enough creatures at Green Meadows.

But oh – there was the old pigeon house – it could
easily be mended; and Green Meadows would once more
have its fantail pigeons flying round, and their cooing
would echo round the old house as it had done years ago.

Granny nodded. 'All right, I'll take them. Come up
this evening and I'll show you where we have an old
pigeon house. You can mend it, and we'll use that – but
listen! Don't say a word to anyone! I'll meet you at the
back gate about six o'clock!'

That evening, after tea, Granny tried cautiously to find
out where everyone would be at six o'clock. She was now
feeling very guilty about the pigeons. She knew that her
love for animals and birds was rather running away with
her common sense. Goodness, Green Meadows was
becoming quite a menagerie! And oh dear, it was
dreadful of her not to tell Mother!

'Not to tell my own daughter! What's come over me?'
thought Granny. 'I'm a bad old woman! Still – I'll see
what happens. I *know* everyone will love the pigeons –
the pretty, pretty things!'

There was a Scout meeting at half-past five, and Clare

and Sam were going to a party. How very fortunate! She would be able to see the pigeon-man in safety. Granny disappeared that afternoon and went to have a look at the fallen-down wooden house, with its six little doorways at the top for pigeons to go in and out. Yes, a strong man could easily mend that. But it would need two people to erect it.

'I'll ask Sid,' thought Granny. Sid was a great standby. He not only worked a lot in the garden, which was beginning to look much tidier, but he was always ready to do any jobs too. In fact, he considered himself as one of the family now, and thought the world of Mother.

The coast was quite clear at six o'clock and Granny slipped down to the back gate. Pam and Sue had taken their puppy for his daily lessons, and Ronnie had fed his rabbit, cleaned the cage, and gone. Nobody was about at all.

The pigeon-man was waiting at the gate. He lifted his cap to Granny. She took him to the stables, feeling that was a safe place to talk.

'What's your name?' she asked.

'Joe Silver,' he said. 'I'm an odd-jobman, and I go out by the day, gardening, or mending fences – well, I do anything really. And I keep pigeons; always have done, since I was so high! Some folks are mad on dogs or cats or horses. I'm mad on pigeons.'

'I used to be too,' said Granny. 'They came and fed out of my hand – they sat on my shoulders and head. They . . .'

'That's right! Mine do the same with me!' said Joe

Silver. 'Well, these I've got are all my own breeding – I had them from eggs. They're white fantails. I never thought I wouldn't be allowed to keep them when I got that little house down on the estate. But they're strict there – they say pigeons spoil the roofs or something – and I was to kill all mine.'

'Wicked!' said Granny. 'I'm glad you came to me. Now listen, Joe, I'll take you down to where there's my old pigeon house. It fell down in a gale of wind one night, and there it's been ever since.'

They went down to the corner where the old pigeon house lay. Joe was most impressed. 'It's a beauty!' he said. 'A real good one. I've only got a poor little house – made it myself. I don't reckon you'd have liked it in *your* garden, for the pigeons. I can easily mend this one. My word, my pigeons will think themselves grand to be in a house like this.'

'What are they called?' asked Granny, as Joe began to examine the wooden house on its long pole.

'Snowdrop, Snowball, Snow-White, and Snowflake,' began Joe, 'and there's Coo-Roo and Fanny – short for fantail,' he added, in case Granny didn't know!

'Lovely names,' said Granny. 'Well – I must leave you now. Do you know Sid Miller? He'll be along soon, and you can ask him to give you a hand. He'll tell you where everything is.'

'Er – what about paying you?' asked Joe. 'I can't ask favours if I don't pay for them.'

'I don't want paying, thank you,' said Granny. 'If you mend the old pigeon house, put it up, and lend me your pigeons, that's enough! And, by the way – I'd like you to keep it to yourself that I'm having the pigeons. I'm – er – well, I'm going to surprise the family, you see!'

She walked off, jingling. Joe looked after her respectfully. His pigeons would be safe here! He'd bring their corn himself. Nobody else must feed them, or they'd forget him, and wouldn't come like a white cloud on to his shoulders and head.

He went to find Sid, who was hard at work clearing yet another bed. The rosebeds were now beautifully tidy, and all the roses had been pruned. Other flower-beds were finished too, and Sid had been debating whether he might bring up a few nice plants from the shop and put them in when nobody was looking. The shop sold plants as well as fruit and vegetables, and it was just the time of year to put things in.

'A few delphiniums would be nice at the back,' thought Sid. 'And some columbines there – and I could put a whole mass of forget-me-nots in that corner, where Mrs Marshall could see them from the kitchen window. I've got some beauties at the shop now.'

He was surprised to see Joe Silver. 'Hello,' he said. 'What are *you* doing here?'

Joe told him. Sid listened with great interest, and then told him about Flash the pony.

'The only thing that bothers me is how to pay the old lady,' said Joe. 'What do you pay them for keeping Flash here?'

'This!' said Sid, waving his fork round him. 'I come and garden – I'm tidying it up. See those beds? Well, they were in a forest of weeds. Now look at them. Can't you do something like that in return? They won't take money. It's no good asking them. They're like that.'

'Don't often meet people like that these days,' said Joe. 'Most people take, take, take all the time, and don't give anything. Right. First of all I'll mend the pigeon house, and then I'll get you to give me a hand and put it up. Then I'll have a look round and mend the walls a bit, and the stable doors; and I could paint up the front of the house if they'd let me.'

It was quite extraordinary, but not one of the Marshall family except Granny knew that the pigeon house was being mended. Joe finished the job in two evenings and then he and Sid put it up. It looked fine!

'I'll bring the pigeons along tomorrow,' said Joe. 'I'll have to wire them into the house for a week, so that they get used to this for their new home, else they'll all fly back to me. Give me a hand with them, will you, Sid?'

It was Sam who discovered that the pigeon house was up – and that there were six white pigeons wired into it! The wire netting enclosed the top of the house like a cage. The pigeons could get out on the ledge round the house and go in and out of their holes, but they couldn't fly away.

Sam stared in utter amazement. Then he tore indoors. 'Mother! Mother! There are pigeons in the pigeon house – and it's up again! But, Mother, somebody's been cruel. They're all wired in, they can't fly into the air!'

Mother rushed out, followed by Francis and Clare. Well, well – Sam was right. The pigeon house was up, and pigeons strutted about on the ledge!

'Rookity-coo,' said one, in his pretty cooing voice. 'Rookity-coo-coo-coo!'

'Oh, Mother!' cried Clare in delight. 'Where did they come from! Oh, aren't they lovely! Look, they spread their tails out just like a fan.'

'Oh, *now* I know why they're called fantails,' said Sam, pleased. 'But who put them there? Mother, it's cruel to wire them in, isn't it?'

'No, dear – not if they've just been put there,' said his mother. 'They have to get used to their new home, you see. The wire stops them from flying away. Now – I have a feeling that Granny's behind all this! She's been looking rather *peculiar* these last few days – a kind of guilty look. I believe it's a surprise for us.'

They went to tackle Granny. 'Those lovely pigeons!' said Mother. 'What do you know about them, Granny? Oh, the pretty things! How glorious they will look flying about Green Meadows! Where *did* they come from?'

A great load rolled off Granny's mind. Mother was pleased. She *liked* pigeons – oh, what a relief! Granny beamed.

'Well,' she said, 'I suppose it *is* a kind of surprise. But actually I kept it a secret because I thought you mightn't want pigeons, but I hoped that when you once saw them flying about, clapping their white wings in the air, you would love them! I'm a bad old woman. I thought you might not say yes at first – but I wanted them so badly that *I* said yes, without telling you!'

'Granny's naughty! Granny, you look as if you know

you're naughty!' said Sam in delight. 'Are you?'

'Yes, I am,' said Granny. 'Now stop it, Sam – you are hugging me like a bear. Goodness me, what I'll do when you're a bit bigger I don't know! There won't be anything of me left. Well – you like the pigeons then?'

There wasn't any doubt of that – and they liked them even more when Joe at last took away the wire and they flew into the air, rookity-cooing and clapping their white wings in glee. Then down they came like great snowflakes, and settled on the grass, fluffing out their feathers, and holding their pretty heads proudly.

They were soon ready to perch on anyone's head and shoulders, and Sam was delighted when one day he had the whole six on him! Mother grew used to having one or two on the kitchen windowsill, watching her at work. She loved their cooing.

Daddy liked them too. He sat out in the sun in his wheelchair, and the pigeons flew down to him, settling on his shoulders and knees. Really, they were a great success.

Joe was a great success too! He was a born handyman and liked nothing better than to mend this and strengthen that, and paint here and creosote there. Mother let him. She saw that he was happy and hard-working and intensely grateful to the family for taking his beloved pigeons. He promised that the first three pigeon eggs to hatch should belong to the three children.

The holidays came to an end. Francis wandered round the garden with his mother. It was the beginning of May, and the lilac bushes were out, scenting the air. Francis looked round.

'You know, Mother,' he said, 'Green Meadows is looking very different from how it was when we walked round in February, and saw the first snowdrop! See how tidy and trim it is! All the beds cleared – and Sid's cut the grass twice with the old mower that Joe mended.'

'Yes,' said his mother. 'It's *quite* different. Joe's done such a lot, and Sid's a real wonder. He ought to have been a gardener, no doubt about that. He's got green fingers – everything grows for him!'

'It's only you, Mother, that things are still hard for,' said Francis, struck by his mother's pale face. 'Are you doing too much? You're not ill, are you?'

'No, darling,' said Mother. 'Just tired. Dear old Granny is so happy with the animals and one thing and another that she can't help me so much – and holidays always mean more work – and Daddy doesn't seem to get any better. I just feel a bit tired and worried, that's all. Oh, for a nice little house, a *tiny* little house – and yet I couldn't bear to leave this lovely garden!'

'You rang the first snowdrop for luck – but it hasn't brought *you* much luck, Mother,' said Francis. 'Look – I found a four-leaved clover today – that's one of the luckiest things there is. It's for you. Now just see if things don't get better for you!'

He pressed the little four-leaved clover into her hand. She laughed. 'I'll put it under my pillow tonight,' she said. 'Then we'll see what luck it brings.'

9
A New Pet – and a Shock!

One day, two weeks after the children had gone back to school, a young man came to see Mother. He was dressed in chauffeur's uniform and looked very smart. He saluted Mother and asked if he could see Francis.

'He hasn't come back from school yet,' she said. 'What do you want him for? You can leave a message for him if you like.'

'Well, it's like this,' said the young man. 'I live near the new housing estate – not far from Joe Silver – and I've got a dog.'

Mother knew what was coming then, of course! She smiled. 'Go on,' she said.

'Well – I wondered if you'd let your boy have the dog here,' said the young man.

'Aren't you allowed to keep him, then?' said Mother.

'Oh yes – but the neighbours don't like him,' said the young man. 'He's big, you see, and he sometimes wants to play with the children. If he's a bit rough, he almost knocks them down, he's so big. So I've had to keep him chained up, and he howls the place down. My neighbour's been to the police about him and . . .'

'Did you keep him chained up all the time? said

Mother. 'Not on a short chain surely?'

'Yes. I had to,' said the young man. 'I tell you, the neighbours were downright nasty about him. His name's Duke. He's an Alsatian, and a beauty.'

'And what is your name? And where do you work?' asked Mother. 'You're a chauffeur, aren't you?'

'Yes. My name's Harrison, Bill Harrison – and I'm chauffeur to Sir Giles Heston-Baker,' said the young man. 'Actually I live in the lodge by the gates of Harrow Manor, where Sir Giles lives; but the housing estate stretches right up to there. I think the people are jealous because they are not allowed to keep dogs or chickens on the estate, and I can keep both, though I'm almost on the edge of it.'

'I see,' said Mother. 'Well – bring the dog along this evening and I'll let my son see him. You'll have to provide his food, of course. A big dog like that must eat a lot.'

'Yes,' said Harrison. 'I'd like to pay something too, but Joe Silver tells me you won't take payment. Is that right?'

'Quite right,' said Mother. 'Well – you'll be along this evening, then?'

Bill arrived that evening with Duke. He was on a short lead, and was a big powerful dog, very handsome indeed. He pulled vigorously at the lead, and Bill had hard work to keep him at his side.

'Oh! What a beautiful dog!' said Clare, and went to pat him. To her enormous surprise, he growled. She stepped back in alarm.

'It's all right,' said Bill. 'He just doesn't know you, that's all. He has to be introduced. Duke – friends, Duke, friends. All friends!' And Bill patted the three children on the back. Duke watched, his tongue hanging out, his eyes wary. Then he suddenly wagged his big tail.

'There! Now he knows you and he'll always be your friend,' said Bill. 'Shake, Duke!'

Duke offered a paw, just as Rex had done, and the children shook it, though Clare was a little scared. No dog had ever growled at her before.

'He's laughing,' said Sam. 'Look!' And, indeed it did look exactly as if Duke were laughing, for his mouth was wide open, and he showed his teeth as if he were smiling. His tail waved to and fro.

'Will he get on all right with the other animals?' asked Francis, anxiously. 'He's so big he could almost eat them up!'

'Well – not at first. He'll have to get used to them,' said Bill. 'Have you got a yard anywhere? He'll have to be chained up, or he'll run away. And he can jump like anything – over the highest wall! He can go halfway up a tree too.'

'Goodness!' said Clare, looking at Duke with much respect. 'Is he valuable?'

'Very,' said Bill. 'Actually I'm looking after him for my master, Sir Giles Heston-Baker, who's away for a bit. I've had him with me so much I almost feel he's mine – but he's not really.'

Dan came up the path and Duke growled and snarled. Dan backed away in alarm.

'Tell Duke it's Dan, quickly,' said Clare. 'I don't like him when he looks like that.'

So Dan was introduced and shook paws, and was relieved to see Duke's tail waving in a most friendly manner.

'You see,' said Bill, 'the kids on the housing estate don't like Duke, and they tease him. They shout at him and throw stones at him, and he nearly goes mad, because he's on a chain and can't get free.'

'Throw stones at him! No wonder he won't be friendly at first when he sees children!' said Francis, indignantly. 'It isn't his fault if he's not friendly. I expect he thinks *we* might throw stones at him. We wouldn't, Duke. You can trust us.'

Duke's tail waved again, and once more he opened his mouth, hung out his tongue and looked as if he were laughing.

'Except for Rex, he's the handsomest dog I've ever seen,' said Dan. 'Have we really got to keep him on a chain?'

'We can have a run-wire,' said Francis. 'We'll make him a nice big run down in the orchard where Flash is. We'll string a wire from one tree to another, and fasten his chain to that, so that he can run about a lot, as much as he likes, but the wire will keep him from running away, or attacking anyone he doesn't know.'

'That's a good idea,' said Bill. 'I hadn't heard of a run-wire. He's always been on his short chain – this one, see – and I tell you, he sometimes nearly went mad, especially when I had to leave him and take the car and go off for the day somewhere.'

'It's enough to make a dog really vicious,' said Francis. 'You shouldn't have done that. All right, we'll have him. Let's go down to the orchard straight away, and find a good place for him.'

Duke was soon running up and down on a run-wire in the orchard. Bill went off and came back with a huge supply of meat for him, and promised to come each day to take him for a long walk. Flash the pony was most interested in this big, energetic dog, running up and down the wire. He wandered up and bent down his head to sniff at him. Duke growled; but Flash went on sniffing, and then gave a little whinny.

Duke's tail began to wag slowly. He put out his tongue and licked Flash's nose. Clare was watching near by and she laughed. 'They're friends!' she said. 'Flash, *you* weren't afraid of his growl, were you? He's been badly treated, Flash so you must be kind to him.'

Duke settled in. He didn't howl, and the only person he barked at was the dustman. 'That's because he sees the dustman come in with empty hands, and go out with the dustbin – and he thinks he's robbing us!' said Mother. 'We can't cure him of that!'

One evening Rita came to see her kitten, which had now grown much bigger, and had a lovely coat. She found Dapple playing in the orchard near Duke, who was lying down with Flash the pony beside him. The two were great friends. Duke had Rex's old kennel, because Rex now slept in the house, promoted to a fine basket, bought for him by Dan. Clare said that if only Flash could get into Duke's kennel, the two of them, dog and pony, would sleep there side by side!

Rita caught up her kitten and hurried away, holding it tightly. Francis saw her. 'Whatever's the matter?' he said.

'*Please* don't let Dapple go near Duke,' begged Rita. 'I met Joan and Dick today, who live near where Bill Harrison lives, and they told me that Duke chases cats and kittens, and once he nearly bit a kitten's tail off.'

'I don't believe it,' said Francis. 'He was always kept on a chain. Bill said so.'

'But he used to escape sometimes,' said Rita. 'He used to break his chain. He attacked cats and dogs – and he bit a little girl one day, and another time he bit a boy. Dick said he goes quite mad sometimes, when he breaks his chain. Nobody's safe then.'

Francis laughed. He was fond of Duke, and could handle him well now. Even Clare had forgotten her first little scare. As for Sam, he rolled over and over on the grass with Duke, who pounced on him, pretended to worry him and reduced Sam to squeals of laughter. He even liked Duke better than Rex!

But the twins, Pam and Sue, came with the same story two days later. 'You be careful of Duke,' said Pam. 'The milkman told our mother that he's fierce, and they warned us not to go too near him. He's already bitten two or three people.'

'I don't believe it,' said Francis. 'A dog is only allowed one bite.'

'Well, you be careful,' said Sue. 'The milkman said

that sometimes he goes quite crazy, breaks his chain and tears off to see if he can find his *real* master, Sir Giles. And it's then he turns and bites anyone in his way. You be careful.'

Francis said nothing of this to the others. He thought it might upset them, and Clare might even believe it and be frightened of Duke. He wondered how it was that the stories got about? Surely there wasn't really any truth in them? Duke *couldn't* behave like that!

But one day something unpleasant happened. The three children had gone for a picnic with their mother and Granny. Daddy was left in his wheelchair in the garden. All the animals were either shut up in their cages, or safe in the orchard. The pigeons sat on their pigeon house in the bright sun, and cooed to one another, kissing with their beaks.

Four children came by. They heard the pigeons cooing and looked over the wall. They saw the orchard, with Flash the pony pulling peacefully at the grass under the trees. They saw Duke!

He had heard them coming and he was sitting up watchfully, his pointed ears pricked.

'Coo, look! That's Duke, isn't it! You know, the big Alsatian Bill Harrison used to have, chained up in his yard!' said a boy.

'Is he chained?' said a girl, cautiously. 'He's fierce, you know. I've seen him snarl like anything.'

'Yes. He's chained,' said another boy. 'Listen – he's growling. Yah! You can't get at us! Brrrrr! Yoo-hoo!'

Duke got up angrily and growled again. The boy

picked up a stone and sent it whizzing at him. It struck the dog on his back and made him jump. He growled again, then snarled, showing all his gleaming white teeth. The girls were scared and ran away, but the two boys stayed there, grinning.

'Yoo-hoo! Silly dog! Ugly dog! Brrrrrr!'

They threw more stones, and Duke ran up and down his run-wire, trying his hardest to get free. He barked and barked. Daddy heard him, and, using his hands on the wheels of his chair, he turned them and ran the chair slowly down to the orchard. Whatever was the matter with Duke?

He was just in time to see a boy hurl a large stone at the dog. It hit him on the head. Duke went completely crazy, racing up and down the run-wire, tugging at his chain, almost choking himself. The boys saw Mr Marshall and fled. And a very good thing they did, because there was a sudden *snap*. The wire broke, and Duke found himself free. His chain was still on him, trailing beside him – but he was free!

He leapt straight over the wall and disappeared, barking wildly. Mr Marshall didn't know what to do. He couldn't get out of his chair because he couldn't walk by himself. He could only wait for the others to come home, and Bill had taken the car to fetch them.

The children, their mother, and Granny came home sunburnt and tired, after a lovely picnic. Rex danced along beside them. He was never tired! Sam was whistling loudly.

As soon as they got to the gate they heard their father

calling them. 'There's Daddy shouting – quick – run and see if anything's the matter,' said Mother.

The children ran – and were surprised to see their father's chair in the orchard. He had stayed there, hoping that Duke would come back. But he hadn't.

He told them what had happened. Clare wept bitterly, and the corners of Sam's mouth went right down.

'Poor Duke,' wept tender-hearted Clare. 'Those hateful, hateful children! Where's he gone, Daddy?'

Daddy didn't know. 'He'll come back,' he said. 'Don't worry.'

But Francis worried very much. He remembered those tales he had heard. Duke had now been tormented again – and he might well go crazy and bite somebody. Then that would be the end of him. He was very quiet as he ate his supper with the others.

Clare kept crying, till Granny got quite cross. 'What good do tears do?' she said. 'You make us all miserable, Clare. Do stop now.'

'She's tired,' said Mother. 'We all are after our long walk and lovely picnic. Off to bed now – Granny and I will wash up.'

'I've just got to go out and see that all the animals are all right,' said Francis. He went out into the evening. It was still light. He walked down to the orchard, and Flash came towards him. He put his big head on the boy's shoulder and stood quite still while Francis talked to him and fondled him.

'What's happened to Duke?' asked Francis. 'I wish you could tell me. I'm so worried, Flash. You see, if he gets crazy with anger, he might bite somebody, and then we would never see him again.'

Flash whinnied; he couldn't tell the boy anything. He had been scared and upset himself when the stones had been thrown and he had galloped away frightened when he head Duke barking and tearing up and down.

Francis left the pony in the sweet-smelling orchard and went slowly up to bed. Sid had come as usual to do what he called his 'spot of gardening', and Mother had asked him to call at the police station and see if there was any news about Duke, and to leave a message at Bill's cottage, at the gates of Harrow Manor. There didn't seem anything else to do except to wait and see if Duke came back.

Francis couldn't sleep that night. He lay tossing and turning, worrying about Duke. Had he bitten someone? Would he be taken to the police station if so? Would they ever see him again? It wasn't Duke's fault. Those hateful boys! They ought to be punished. So his thoughts went, on and on.

He heard his mother come up, and he got out of bed and went to the door. 'Mother! Are you going to bed?'

'Yes, it's late, dear,' said his mother. 'You ought to be asleep. You're not worrying about Duke, are you?'

'Yes. Have you heard any news of him?' asked Francis.

'A little. Sid came up to say that Duke had been seen tearing down the road towards Bill's cottage. But he isn't there. It's in darkness, and Bill isn't back. He won't be home till late, Sid says.'

'Oh,' said Francis. 'Perhaps he's somewhere there waiting for Bill. Mother – has he bitten anyone? I did hear that he bit people when he was furious.'

'I didn't hear,' said Mother. 'But it's enough to make a dog bite when he's tormented as he was. Daddy says quite a large stone struck him on the head.'

'I know. I keep thinking he may have a horrid cut there,' said Francis. 'Well – goodnight, Mother, and thank you for the lovely picnic. It *was* nice to have you out for the whole afternoon like that.'

'Goodnight, dear,' said Mother and kissed him. 'Sleep well! Maybe Duke will be back in the orchard in the morning.'

Francis got into bed. He waited till his mother had put her light out. He heard the click, and then he got up and dressed himself. He was going to Bill's cottage to find Duke! Perhaps he was hiding somewhere near there. Francis was sure he would come if he called him.

He slipped down the stairs and out of the garden door. It was bright moonlight, and he could see everything almost as clearly as in the daytime. He sped down the garden and into the lane.

It was only about ten minutes' walk to Bill's. Francis ran most of the way until he saw the big burly form of Mr Streetly, the village policeman. He hid in the hedge at once. Mr Streetly would be sure to send him straight back home – and he must find Duke, he must!

He crept out of the hedge when the policeman had gone by. He was soon at the gates of Harrow Manor. He came to Bill's cottage, on the right-hand side of the gates.

It was in darkness. Bill wasn't back yet then.

'Duke!' called Francis, softly. 'Duke, old boy! Where are you? It's me, Francis. I've come to find you, Duke! Duke! Duke!'

But no Duke came, and not a sound stirred anywhere. Not even the trees moved, for there was not a breath of wind. Francis went through the open gates of Harrow Manor and walked a little way up the drive.

'Duke!' he called, and whistled the little familiar whistle that the dog had grown to know and obey. 'Duke!'

There was no sign of the dog. Francis went on walking up the drive in the clear moonlight. 'Duke! Duke! Come here, old boy! Poor old boy!'

And then at last he heard a sound. What was it? He called again. 'Duke!'

The sound came again – a growl! Francis stopped dead and listened. 'Duke!'

'Grrrrr!' Yes, it *was* a growl – but surely, surely Duke wouldn't growl at a boy who loved him. The growl seemed to come from a small summerhouse not far off. Francis went cautiously towards it. It was not far from the drive itself. He called again. 'Duke, old boy!'

No answer. Francis walked quietly over the little stretch of grass to the summerhouse. The moon shone right into it. Francis stood at the doorway and looked in.

Duke was there! He crouched right at the back, his eyes gleaming in the moonlight, his upper lip curled back and his teeth showing white. He snarled at Francis.

The boy stood still, shocked. He had never seen Duke

look like that before. The dog looked cruel, wicked, vicious – and this was the same Duke he had fondled that morning, and who had licked him and loved him!

'Duke!' said Francis, helplessly. 'Come here, old boy. Don't look like that!'

Duke crept a step forward, crouching low to the ground as if he were going to leap like a cat. He snarled again, and Francis stepped back in panic.

'He means to bite me!' he thought. 'He's going to pounce – and I'm all alone here! He must have bitten others, after all, when he was just like this.'

He was too afraid to stay. He backed away slowly, followed by growls. But Duke didn't rush out of the door as Francis had half-expected. The boy reached the drive and found tears running down his face. He brushed them away. He never, never cried – never! He was a Scout, and he thought himself brave. But after all he wasn't. But oh, Duke! What was to happen to him?

He heard a sudden noise and stopped. It was the sound of a car racing up the drive. It must be Bill bringing his master back! Bill would know what to do, Bill would go in and get Duke out! Francis stood in the middle of the drive as the car came up, waving frantically.

The car stopped suddenly, and Bill leapt out. 'What's up? Francis, what's the matter?'

'It's Duke. Some children tormented him today and he broke the wire and ran off, half-crazy. He's in the summerhouse, growling, and I'm afraid of him,' said Francis, with a gulp. 'He looks so awful – not a bit like himself. Oh, Bill, come and get him, I'm sure he's hurt.'

'What's all this?' said a voice from the back of the car. Bill ran to the back window and spoke to Sir Giles, his master. He told him quickly what Francis had said. Sir Giles got out of the car at once.

'Duke in the summerhouse! Half-crazy! I can't believe it! He was always the gentlest, best-tempered of dogs! What's been happening to him since I've been away? We'll go and get the poor fellow. He'll be beside himself with joy to see me!'

But Duke wasn't. He didn't seem pleased to see either Bill or Sir Giles. In fact, he growled so ferociously at them both that the two men stepped very hurriedly indeed from the doorway.

'Duke!' said Sir Giles and Bill, at the same time. But Duke would not come, and still lay and snarled.

'Look here – the dog's dangerous,' said Sir Giles. 'He'll have to be shot before he does somebody damage. What a pity! Such a beautiful, sweet-tempered dog too! What's changed him into that snarling brute?'

'Shot!' said Francis in utmost horror. 'What do you mean, sir? Shoot old Duke? It isn't his fault. He was teased and tormented till he went half-crazy. He'll be all right tomorrow. I'll stay here all night, somewhere in the bushes near by. You *can't* shoot him!'

'My dear boy, don't upset yourself,' said Sir Giles. 'What's he to do with you, anyway? And what are you doing here at this time of night? Good gracious me, what a peculiar affair this is! You go home, my lad – this dog has got to be shot.'

'But sir – he's hurt. I know he is,' said Francis. 'And

when dogs are hurt they get frightened and snarl and growl, even at their friends. I don't believe he'd really bite either you or Bill – and, after all, he belongs to you. Couldn't you – couldn't you *possibly* go in and pat him or something?'

'I wouldn't dream of it,' said Sir Giles. 'I'd be scared stiff. No, he must be shot, and as soon as possible. He's dangerous.' Francis said no more. He was so upset and troubled he hardly knew what he was doing. He went softly back to the summerhouse. Sir Giles called him sharply, 'Come here, you little idiot.'

Duke was in there, crouching as before. Why was he in such a strange position? The boy's keen eyes searched the dog's body. Then he gave a cry.

'Oh, poor old Duke! You've got your chain twisted all round your hind legs! It's cutting into them. Let me free you, Duke, poor old Duke!'

And the boy went right into the little house and knelt down by the growling dog. 'Dear Duke, poor Duke – let me see the chain. Don't be afraid, it's me, and you know I love you. Poor old Duke, never mind, old boy, I'll put you right. *You* wouldn't bite me, Duke, would you – you're just frightened and in pain. There – move over a bit. Poor old Duke!'

Sir Giles and Bill were staring in amazement into the summerhouse. Francis had made Duke move over a little and was trying to disentangle the chain from the dog's hind legs. It had got wound round and round them, binding them together and cutting into them.

Duke gave a little whine, and then put out his tongue

and licked Francis. The boy's heart turned over with happiness. 'I won't let you be shot,' he said. 'Don't you worry, Duke! I'll stay with you all night – don't you be afraid!'

10

Well Done, Francis!

Once the cruel chain was unwound from his bleeding legs, Duke tried to get up. He just managed to stand and then fell down again. 'He's hurt,' called Francis, his voice trembling. 'He's all right now – he's licking me. He was only frightened; he didn't know why his back legs were locked together.'

Sir Giles went cautiously into the summerhouse. Duke whined in pleasure and tried to get up, but fell down again. He licked his master lovingly. When Bill came in he licked him too.

'There you are, you see,' said Francis, overjoyed. 'He's not dangerous. He's just a poor hurt dog. You won't shoot him, will you?'

'You're really a most extraordinary boy,' said Sir Giles, with wonder in his voice. 'And just about the bravest I've ever seen. That dog might have flown at you and bitten you badly. Poor old Duke! You'll never have a better friend than this boy here tonight!'

'You won't shoot him, will you?' said Francis again. 'You haven't said you won't.'

'I certainly won't,' said Sir Giles, who was now kneeling down beside Duke, examining his legs. 'These wounds want seeing to – there's one very bad one on this left leg.'

'Oh, what a pity the Animal Van isn't near,' said Francis. 'The Animal Doctor – the vet there would turn out of bed to see to him. I know he would.'

'You needn't worry,' said Sir Giles, 'I'm a surgeon – and if I can see to the wounds of humans, I can certainly see to the wounds of a dog. Bill, can you carry him indoors?'

Bill could and did, and Duke allowed him to pick him up, heavy as he was, and take him up the drive. Sir Giles unlocked the front door and went in. 'You'd better go home, son,' said Sir Giles, kindly. 'I'll come and see you tomorrow and we'll have a talk about this. I'm going to tell your father all about it. I wish I had a son like you!'

'Please don't send me home,' said Francis. 'Let me stay here and be with Duke.'

'You are a most persistent young man,' said Sir Giles, with a laugh. 'All right. Bill, take the car and go and tell this boy's people he's all right and will be home in the morning. Or wait a bit – have you a telephone in your house, my boy?'

'No,' said Francis, happy again. Now he could stay with Duke and get him absolutely right again – no more snarling, no more growling, no more threats of shooting!

Bill went off. A wooden trestle table was put up quickly and Duke was lifted gently on to it. Sir Giles took off his coat, rolled up his sleeves, and set to work.

Duke was as good as gold. Francis was told to talk to him and stroke and pat him while the surgeon cleaned up the wounds and bandaged deftly. There was a wound on his head too, where the stone had struck him. 'Nothing much,' said Sir Giles, 'but enough to make a dog very angry. There, my boy – he's finished. Do you really want to stay with him tonight?'

'You said I could,' said Francis. 'Will Duke be able to walk all right after this? His legs were rather bad, weren't they?'

'Oh, he'll be all right,' said Sir Giles. 'Look – he's trying to stand on them now. Up you get, Duke – that's right. See, he's even walking a few steps, though it must hurt him!'

Duke and Francis went to sleep together. The butler put a pile of rugs in a corner of a small study for Duke and made up a couch for Francis to sleep on. But as soon as the door closed Francis was off the couch and cuddled down by Duke. The dog licked his face and whined. In half a minute both dog and boy were asleep.

Francis was awakened in the morning by Duke licking his face all over. He sat up, rubbing his eyes. 'Goodness, Duke! I shan't need to wash my face at all if you go on like that! How are your legs? Do you feel better?'

Duke felt fine. His legs felt stiff, but he was in no pain. He walked a few steps. His right hind leg wasn't too bad, so he lifted his left one and carried it off the ground, running round the room on three legs.

Francis was delighted. 'You'll be all right, Duke! Isn't Sir Giles clever? How did you get that chain all round them – it must have swung round as you ran and tied itself tightly so that it lamed you. Never mind. Your master is back, and you're all right!'

There was a knock at the study door, and the butler came in. 'Good morning,' he said. 'I've been sent by Sir Giles to see if you're all right – and would you like a bath, sir? You were so tired last night that we didn't bother to worry you about washing or undressing or anything.'

'Well – I *am* rather dirty,' said Francis, looking down at himself. His knees were black! His hair was on end and his face was extremely dirty. 'I suppose it's crawling about in that summerhouse.'

'A very dusty place,' said the butler. Francis felt rather scared of him. He was so very stiff and correct! Then, quite suddenly, he unbent.

'Bill Harrison says you went into that summerhouse when Duke was raving mad!' he said. 'He says he and Sir Giles wouldn't go near him – and Sir Giles was just going to have him shot. Is that right?'

'Well – he wasn't raving mad, nothing like it,' said Francis. 'He was just terrified because he'd got his legs all wound up with his chain – and he'd lamed himself trying to run like that with the chain biting into him. He's all right now – look at him!'

'You're a caution, that's what you are,' said the butler. 'I wouldn't go near a snarling dog for anything in the world. Come along, and get into that bath. You can't have breakfast with Sir Giles, looking as dirty as that.'

'Goodness – am I to have breakfast with him?' said Francis, startled. 'I'd better hurry up and have a bath then. What a pity my clothes are so dirty too.'

When he was taken into a most magnificent bathroom,

he looked at himself in a long mirror there. 'Gracious, I look like a beggar boy! Whatever would Granny say?'

He hopped into a steaming bath, and soaped himself well, even washing his hair. An enormous thick snowy-white towel hung ready for him on a warm rail. It covered him from head to foot when he got out of the bath, and trailed on the floor.

There was a knock on the door. 'Master Francis, breakfast is ready when you are. I'll wait in the hall and take you in. I'll brush and shake your clothes if you'll hand them out.'

Francis opened the door and handed them out. He dried himself well and smoothed his hair down. Soon the door opened and his clothes were handed back. They looked quite different now, though they were still rather dirty.

He went down into the great hall, feeling clean and very hungry. Duke was waiting there for him, and the butler too. They were taken in state to a pleasant morning room, where Sir Giles was already seated at breakfast.

'Good morning!' he said. 'I hope you slept well and feel hungry for your breakfast. There are sausages, bacon, or eggs – or all three together!'

Francis had a wonderful breakfast with Sir Giles. Duke sat close beside him, putting his head on the boy's knee at times. Sir Giles asked Francis quite a lot of questions, and the boy talked away frankly about his family.

'There's Granny – she adores animals! Our house,

Green Meadows, belongs to her, but she won't sell it even though it's much too big, and we're too poor to use even half the rooms. It's got a lovely garden, very very big – and stables, which we just use as a junk place! Then there's Daddy – well, Daddy isn't very lucky. He has to live in a wheelchair, and . . . '

'What's the matter with him?' asked Sir Giles.

'I don't really know,' said Francis. 'He was hurt in the last war, in the back – I don't remember that of course – and he had lots of treatment, but nothing seems to do any good. His legs don't seem any use. That's why he has to be in a wheelchair. But he's very cheerful. And he's got lots of medals – one very special one for great bravery.'

'Well, I should like to tell him that he's got a son who also deserves a medal for great bravery,' said Sir Giles. 'So I'll run you down in the car, and we'll have a word with him together. I sent a message to your mother last night to say you were safe here with me. She was very surprised, of course.'

'What about Duke?' asked Francis. 'Don't let Bill have him – the children tease him so, and he's chained up in Bill's small garden. I had a run-wire for him in our orchard.'

'Would you like him to go back with you?' asked Sir Giles. 'I would take it as a very great kindness if you would have him. I shall be out a lot, and Bill, who as you know is my chauffeur, will be with me. I don't want the dog left alone.'

'I'd love to have him!' said Francis, eagerly. 'And I could see to his legs, if you'd show me how to. I'm going to be a vet, an animal doctor, when I grow up. I'd like to run one of those big Animal Vans – you know, the ones belonging to the P.D.S.A.'

'Are all your family like you?' asked Sir Giles amused.

'Well – we're all animal-lovers, if that's what you mean,' said Francis puzzled. 'Or do you mean are they all like me to look at?'

'No. I didn't mean that,' said Sir Giles. 'I only thought that if all your family were like you, they must be a very nice family. Now, you work that out, while I go and get my coat and hat. We'll go down to Green Meadows straight away. Take Duke to the car. Let him walk if he wants to.'

Soon they were all on the way to Green Meadows, driven by Bill, who was very glad to see that Duke seemed so much better. They came to the gate and Francis jumped out of the car and held open the door for Sir Giles before Bill could. Francis thought the surgeon was a wonderful man. While he had been waiting for him with Duke, Bill had told him that Sir Giles was one of the cleverest surgeons in the whole country.

It was Saturday, so everyone was at home. Dan and Rita, Pam and Sue were there too, looking after their pets, and so were Ronnie and Harry.

Granny was the first to welcome Sir Giles, for she was in the orchard near by with Flash the pony. Sir Giles raised his hat as Francis introduced them.

'This is my granny,' he said.

'Good morning,' said Sir Giles. 'You seem to keep a kind of Animals' Home here!'

'I only wish it was!' said Granny smiling. 'But we've only a few creatures really! Well, Francis? Another adventure – what a boy you are to be sure!'

They all went into the house. Mother and Daddy were in the sitting room, and Daddy was just being helped into the wheelchair.

'Good morning, Mr Marshall,' said Sir Giles 'I've come to have a few words with you – about your son.'

But it wasn't a *few* words they had that morning; it was a long long talk – a talk that had the most surprising and unexpected results!

After the talk was over, and Sir Giles had gone. Mother and Granny turned to each other in excitement. Francis saw tears in his mother's eyes.

'He said he could do something to John's back!' said Mother.

'He said he might walk again, in a few months' time!' said Granny, sniffing, and trying to find her hanky.

'He only said might, you know,' said Daddy, who looked as excited as Mother and Granny. 'We've had so many disappointments over various treatments. This might be another.'

'Oh, but Sir Giles is such a *clever* surgeon,' said Francis. 'He's the best in the country. Bill told me so.'

He sat near his father, with Duke beside him. He felt very happy. He kept remembering the things that Sir Giles had said to his father about him. 'Very great courage. A half-crazed dog, that even Bill and I were afraid of. Boy to be proud of. Like father, like son – and the son deserves a medal too! Wish he was *my* son.

Congratulate you on having a boy like that.'

Mother had cried with pride to hear about it all. Daddy had sat and listened with shining eyes. Granny couldn't keep still, she was so excited, and she had jingled all the time. Yes, Francis was very happy – and to crown it all, Sir Giles had offered to examine Daddy's back, and had said he was almost certain he could do something to make the pain go, and *perhaps* Daddy might hobble about with two sticks.

When Sir Giles had gone, Francis rushed out to the others, and told them the news. Everyone was pleased. and Clare and Sam were full of joy. Dear old Daddy – he did deserve to have a little luck. It wasn't fair that great bravery should be rewarded by great pain and crippled legs.

Of course, they all listened open-mouthed to the tale of the night before. Duke listened open-mouthed too, his tongue hanging out, looking just as if he were smiling. He sat as close to Francis as he could possibly get. He couldn't seem grateful enough to him.

Francis put his arms round the big dog's neck. 'You didn't bite, did you?' he said. 'I love you, dear old Duke, and I wish you were mine! I'd like you!'

Duke licked him, and the others watched enviously. It was quite clear that Duke regarded himself as belonging to Francis, and to no one else.

Sam suddenly stared at Rita. 'You've gone awfully red,' he said. 'Why have you?'

'Well,' said Rita, 'it wasn't true what I told you about Duke. He *hadn't* bitten anyone! It was just a tale made up by the children he had barked at – a sort of excuse for them to throw stones at him. I thought they were telling the truth, but they weren't. I'm sorry about that, Francis.'

Francis felt angry. He turned to the twins, Pam and Sue. ' *You* said the same thing!' he said.

'Yes. The milkman told us,' said Sue. 'But he's always full of tales, and our mother says half of them aren't true. So I expect that wasn't either.'

'So Duke never *has* bitten anyone!' said Francis. He stroked the dog's head, as he lay down close beside the boy. 'And you never will, will you – unless it's somebody wicked who is doing wrong. Oh, I'm glad I went into the summerhouse and saved you last night, Duke. It would have been dreadful to have you shot when you had never bitten anyone, and didn't even bite *me!*'

Sir Giles wasted no time about having a look at Daddy's back. He sent his car for him the very next day, and took him up to his hospital in London. When Daddy came back he was half cheerful, half sad.

'He says there's hope, but I must go to a hospital rather far away, one that specializes in my kind of back,' said Daddy. 'And oh dear – I shan't be back for some months. It's a very long job.'

'Oh, what a pity!' said Mother. 'We'll miss you dreadfully!'

'Will we be able to see you?' asked Granny. Daddy shook his head.

'No. It's too far away and the fare there and back would cost a lot of money. We must just do without each other, all of us, and hope for the best,' he said. 'It will be worth it if it makes me just a bit better! If I could even *dress* myself, it would be something. All these jobs are such a strain on Mother, when she has so much else to do.'

'They're not a strain,' said Mother. 'You know I love doing them. Oh dear – when do you go?'

'In two days' time,' said Daddy. 'Bill is going to take me all the way there in the big car. It's unbelievably kind of Sir Giles.'

'Really great people are always unbelievably kind,' said Granny.

'How are we ever going to pay him?' said Mother, looking worried.

'Francis has arranged that,' said Granny, and Francis and everyone else looked at her in amazement.

'I haven't, Granny,' said Francis. 'I haven't arranged anything! I haven't got any money!'

'You *have* arranged it, all the same,' said Granny, smiling at him. 'Sir Giles told me that he's so grateful to you for saving Duke from being shot, and for being willing to look after him and keep him happy, that he's arranged to look after Daddy for you in return!'

'He never told me!' said Francis, amazed.

'I expect he thought you knew,' said Granny. 'He said, "One good turn deserves another", and this is *his* good turn, you see.'

Daddy went off in the big car two days later, lying comfortably on the back seat, waving till he was out of sight. Everyone felt rather mournful when he had gone.

It seemed funny to see the wheelchair with no one sitting patiently in it.

Mother wrote to him every other day. Granny wrote whenever she felt like it, which was quite often. The children wrote each Sunday, just before they went off to Sunday School. And all the animals wrote one day, under Sam's direction!

Daddy got the letter and laughed. On the first page was the imprint of four different-sized paws, and at the bottom Sam had printed:

'Wags from Duke, Rex, Pongo the puppy, and a purr from Mr Black (a loud one).'

On the next page was the imprint of a rabbit's paw, a smaller paw belonging to the guinea pig, and a little paw belonging to Dapple. At the bottom Sam had put: 'A woffle of his nose from Fluffy the rabbit. A wag of Gilbert the guinea pig's tail. (He would wag it if he had one.) And a mew from Dapple.'

On the third page was pinned a long hair, and there were also prints of pigeon feet!

'A hair from Flash's tail (I couldn't get him to put his hoof on the paper). And coos from the pigeons. Do you like the way they have all signed their names, Daddy! I dipped their feet in mud, and pressed them on the paper.'

Daddy laughed when he got that, and put it away carefully to keep. Dear old Sam! Was he still whistling tunelessly? Was Granny still jingling as she walked briskly about? Did Mother look tired and pale, or was she better? Was Clare still flying into hot little tempers and flying out of them again just as quickly? And what about his courageous son, Francis?

Daddy thought of his family over and over again, just as they thought of him. It was a good thing he couldn't see Mother, though! She had gone very thin, and her eyes looked too big for her face, just as Rita's used to do. Francis was very worried about her. He saved her all the work he could; but no matter how much he saved her, there was always more to do, in that big old tumbledown house; doors needed mending, walls painting, floors repairing, and a hundred and one other things!

Joe had done a lot to it, and had made it look gay and pretty – but he couldn't do the big jobs, and there was no money to get anyone else to do them. The garden looked lovely now, for Sid, Dan, and even Bill were working hard in it each evening they could spare. Dan was a fine helper too, and his mother felt pleased, and was very proud when she saw him going off to Scouts' meetings with Francis.

One evening Francis tackled Granny about his mother. 'Granny,' he said, 'is Mother ill? She walks about so slowly, and she looks so sad.'

'She's not well, that's certain,' said Granny. '*I'm* worried about her too, but she won't see the doctor – she's afraid he'll pack her off for a holiday, or send her to bed.'

'Granny, can't you sell Green Meadows, and we'll go somewhere smaller?' said Francis, desperately.

'I don't want to leave it,' said Granny, and she put on her old, obstinate look. 'Good days will come again, and then we'll be glad of a lovely place like this.'

'Good days won't come if Mother gets ill – and how do we know Daddy will come back better, Granny? Oh dear, I wish I was grown up! I'd know better what to do. Granny, let's go and live in the stables! They're not so big as the house!'

'Don't be silly, Francis,' said Granny. ' *Please* don't be silly. It isn't like you to have wild ideas like that. It's more like Clare.'

'Well, it *was* Clare's idea!' said Francis. 'She thought it could be made into a lovely little house, and so it could – and you'd still have the lovely garden, or part of it, at any rate.'

'You are *both* silly,' said Granny. 'Where do you suppose the money is coming from to make the stables into a proper little house?'

'I don't know,' said Frances helplessly. Granny went out of the room, jingling furiously. She was always cross and snappy when she was worried, and she was worried now about Mother, and all the work there was, and what would happen if Mother fell ill – and oh dear, how was John *really* getting on in that faraway hospital?

Francis went to find Duke. He was in the orchard with Flash and Rex. All three ran up to Francis at once, and both dogs leapt up at him. Francis sat down on the grass.

The dogs at once sensed that he was miserable and vied with one another to comfort him. Duke put his head on Francis's shoulder and Rex laid his on the boy's knee. Flash stood above them all, swishing his tail from side to side to keep the summer flies away.

Rex gave a little whine as if to say, 'What's the matter? Tell me.'

'There's nothing much to tell,' said Francis, stroking the silky head. 'Daddy's away, so I'm the man of the family now – but I simply don't know what to do! Mother's ill, I know she is. If something doesn't happen soon, I'll have to ask Sir Giles to lend me the car so that I can go and see Daddy about things – but I don't want to worry him. But nothing nice *will* happen! Things will just go from bad to worse.'

And then, at that very moment, something *did* happen. A car drove slowly by, and suddenly stopped. A window was lowered, and a woman's face looked out.

'This is the place!' she said. 'I'm sure it is. Yes, look – Green Meadows. The old lady must live here. Let's go and see!'

11

'It's a Hap-Hap-Happy Day!'

Francis got up and went to the front gate to see who the visitors were. Two women got out of the car, about his mother's age. They were beautifully dressed. One carried a little dog, and they left a beautiful poodle behind in the car.

'Good evening,' said Francis, politely. 'Did you want to see anyone here?'

'This must be one of the grandchildren!' said the first woman. 'Yes – we have come to see if Mrs Linton is at home. She must be your grandmother, I think.'

'Mrs Linton? Yes, she is my granny,' said Francis. 'Will you come in? I'm Francis, her eldest grandson. Granny is indoors. Who shall I say wants to see her?'

'Tell her it's Ellen Surrey and a friend,' said the visitor and followed Francis up the path.

Francis put them in the sitting room and went to find Granny. His mother was lying down with a headache.

'Granny!' he called. 'Someone to see you. She says her name is Ellen Surrey, and there's a friend with her.'

'Ellen! Ellen Surrey!' cried Granny. 'Oh, what a surprise! She is the daughter of my greatest friend – I've often told you of the little girl whose parents were abroad, and who lived here with my family nearly all her childhood. She loved animals as much as I did. Well, well – to think Ellen is here!'

Granny hurried into the sitting room, and there were exclamations and kisses. Granny called to Francis: 'Darling, get some iced lemonade and some of those little biscuits, will you?'

Francis put the ice into a jug, then the right amount of lemonade and added water. He set out the biscuits on a pretty plate. He was used to doing all kinds of household jobs, and he was as good as Clare at most of them!

'Oooh,' said Sam, appearing, as he always did, when there was any sign of something to eat. 'Who's that for?'

'Not for you,' said Francis. 'Visitors. Get out of my way, Sam, do – and go and see where Dapple is. I've not seen him for ages.'

Sam disappeared. Francis took the biscuits and lemonade into the sitting room. The two visitors and Granny were talking at top speed.

'So this is your eldest grandson,' said Miss Surrey. 'And is he as fond of animals as you are, Aunt Lilian?'

It seemed queer to Francis to hear his granny called Aunt Lilian, but Ellen Surrey had always called her that when she had lived with the family as a little girl. She had known Mother very well indeed too.

'All the children are fond of animals,' said Granny. 'It runs in the family! Your mother was very *very* fond of them – she loved them all. I missed her very much when she went out to South Africa, and I was shocked to hear she had died there not so long ago.'

'Well, you won't be surprised to hear that she left all her money to animals, then,' said Ellen Surrey. 'She knew I had plenty of my own, and in her will she said that she wanted me to buy some place where animals could be kept in peace and happiness: sick animals – injured ones – horses that were too old to work – lost creatures. Well, you knew my mother; she had a place in her heart for any creature in trouble.'

'Yes, I know,' said Granny. 'She was a wonderful woman. It's just like her to want her love for all creatures to continue even when she is dead. Where is this place you have bought? I'd like to come and see it. I'd like to see the animals you have there too. If I were a younger woman I'd have wanted to help!'

'Oh, we haven't bought any place yet,' said Ellen Surrey. 'We've only just got the money, you see. Patricia Hemming, my friend here, is helping me with everything, and she thought it would be nice to have a Home for Animals somewhere in this part of the country. And while we were driving back after seeing over lots of houses today, I suddenly remembered the old place here – Green Meadows – that I loved so much as a child. And I thought I'd come and see if you were still here!'

'And I *am* still here!' said Granny. 'But the place isn't kept up as it was; half the rooms are shut, even the old playroom!'

'But it looks so gay and pretty – and the garden is very well-kept,' said Ellen. 'Isn't it, Patricia?'

They talked and talked and at last they went. Francis had slipped out of the room halfway through the visit, but Granny called him to see the visitors to the gate. He went with them politely and saw them into the car. Ellen Surrey took the wheel, and Patricia Hemming, her friend, leaned out to say goodbye to Francis.

'Goodbye!' she said. 'You know, your granny's house is the *only* one we've seen today that would do for a Home for Animals! It's exactly right, garden and all – but it *would* be just the one we can't have, of course!'

And with a last wave, the two visitors sped away. Sped away before Francis could call them back! Yes, call them back and say, 'Please ask Granny to sell her house! We want a smaller one! *We* know it's a good place to keep animals – we've tried it!'

The boy watched the car speed away. He went into the orchard and sat down beside Duke to think. He was filled with a peculiar excitement. Did Ellen Surrey and her friend really think Green Meadows was just what they wanted? Would Granny sell it if she thought that her friends would have it, and that many creatures would find peace and happiness there, in the house and garden? There was still a small, unbuilt-on field at the back that could be hired for old horses or ponies. Excitement rose still higher in him. He could see it all! The house could also lodge students who wanted training with animals – Miss Surrey had spoken about them too.

Francis got up and walked straight back to the house, Rex and Duke beside him. Dapple dropped down on to his shoulder from a tree branch, a little habit he had. 'That's right,' said Francis. 'Come and back me up!'

Granny was still in the sitting room, putting it tidy.

She looked pleased and excited, for she did not often have visitors.

'Granny,' said Francis, in a suddenly grown-up voice, 'I'm the man of the family now, aren't I? Well, I want you to sit down and listen to me, please. I've got something important to say.'

'Good gracious!' said Granny startled, and sat down at once, jingling loudly. 'Whatever is it?'

'Granny, listen. I think Green Meadows is *exactly* the place that Miss Surrey wants for the Home for Animals,' said Francis. 'Her friend said so. I am sure they would give you a good price for it, especially as Miss Surrey loved it so much when she was a child.'

'Good *gracious* !' said Granny, again.

Francis went on firmly. 'It's a waste of this nice house to have half the rooms shut up, and let the whole place fall to pieces. It's a good thing Sid and Joe and Bill have done so much to make it tidy and neat – for I'm sure Miss Surrey wouldn't want to buy it if she could have seen it a few months ago! So, Granny, I want you to tell her that if she *really* wants Green Meadows, she can have it!'

'But, Francis, dear – where would *we* live?' said Granny. 'I don't think I could bear to go away from here. I know I'm a selfish old woman, but . . .'

'You wouldn't need to go away, Granny,' said Francis, still in his grown-up voice. 'With the money you got for the house and part of the garden, you could easily have the stables made into a darling little house – just the right size for Mother! There are big lofts above the stables, for bedrooms – it could be made beautiful!'

'I've never heard of such a thing!' said Granny, really surprised. 'Anyone would think you were grown up, talking to me like this.'

'Well – *someone's* got to do something,' said Francis desperately, suddenly speaking like a little boy again. 'Because of Mother! Granny, you know you'd love this dear old house to be a home for the creatures you love – and the garden too. Old worn-out horses and donkeys, sick or injured animals, ones who are cast off, unwanted. It's almost a Home for Animals now – we've so many creatures ourselves.'

Granny sat lost in thought. 'I could help with all the animals the Home kept,' she said, her face lighting up. 'And if we *could* have the stables made into a little house, why, we'd be next door to Green Meadows! And we'd keep the bit of garden we love most – the dell, and the flowerbeds, and the bit where the pigeons are.'

'Yes. And we'd have any amount of creatures to play about with,' said Francis, delighted to see that Granny was swinging round to his idea. 'And better than anything – Mother wouldn't have so much to see to in a small house, and nor would you.'

'Fancy you thinking all this out!' said Granny, suddenly looking astonished again. 'Anyone would think you were grown up.'

'Daddy said I was to look after Mother,' said Francis. 'And this is a very good way.'

'I'll talk it over with Mother this very night,' said Granny, looking excited. 'Oh dear – look at the time. Do get Clare in and tell her to help you with the supper. I must see how Mother's headache is.'

When Mother came to supper, with Granny behind her, the headache was quite gone. She looked very cheerful indeed. She went straight up to Francis and kissed him.

'Clever boy!' she said. 'What a wonderful idea! Have you told the others?'

Francis hadn't because he was afraid perhaps his mother would say no to his idea. So they all spent a most excited, and very pleasant, supper talking about future plans. Sam began to whistle loudly.

''*Not* at supper time, Sam,' said Granny, and Sam stopped, only to begin again almost immediately, and this time nobody stopped him. He was very happy and so were they.

The next thing was to ask Miss Surrey if she really would like to have Green Meadows. They had to find out her address, which she hadn't left with them, and then Granny wrote a letter. She wrote it and rewrote it, and spent two whole days over it, nearly driving the family mad!

'Granny! Miss Surrey will buy a house somewhere else if you don't hurry!' said Francis. And that gave Granny such a shock that she finished the letter in a great hurry, and sent Francis out to post it.

Then there came a long wait for an answer. Clare rushed to the door every time the postman came, but no answer arrived. Granny fidgeted about the house, jingling anxiously. Now that she had made up her mind to sell Green Meadows, she couldn't wait.

And then at last a telegraph boy cycled up to the front gate with a telegram. Mother took it and opened it with a trembling hand. She read it out aloud.

'Sorry for delay in answering, but have been away. Delighted to buy Green Meadows. Even more delighted to hear you will be our neighbours. Ellen Surrey.'

Well, what a shout went up! Flash heard it down in the orchard. Duke and Rex heard it and came tearing up to the house. The pigeons heard it and rose into the air in a cloud, clapping their snow-white wings.

'Hurrah! Now we've turned the corner – and things should be all right,' cried Francis. 'What fun we're going to have in the next six months!'

Once Granny made up her mind to sell Green Meadows, she lost no time in pushing things on as quickly as possible. She got a builder to come in and look at the stables, she told Mother to make up her mind exactly how much of the garden she wanted, and she wrote to Daddy to tell him the news.

'I'm delighted!' Daddy wrote back. 'The stables can be converted into a dear little house – they're lovely now, with the old red-brick walls, and red-tiled roof with moss all over it. I'm happy thinking about it, and knowing that you and Mother will be able to have plenty of time there to do all the things you haven't been able to do for so long.'

Daddy's news was rather changeable. One week he sounded very cheerful and much better, and said that he really thought things were going well. The next week he said that he was on his back again, and the treatment had been stopped. Apparently once the right treatment had been found, then things would go well. How he wished he could be at home to share in all the excitement there!

Granny arranged that the builder should get to work at once on the stables, and she and Mother pored over plans that showed all the changes there were to be – windows pulled out and others put in, partitions to be put up for bedrooms in the loft, a kitchen made here, and a larder there.

'I'll like having a bedroom in the loft,' said Clare. 'I'll imagine horses down below, stamping and swishing their tails.'

'I'm going to have a bedroom of my own,' said Sam, pleased. 'The tiniest you ever saw. I won't be sleeping with you any more, Francis.'

'Good thing,' said Francis. 'You won't wake me up with your whistling every morning. Mother, can't you teach Sam to whistle a tune? I've tried, but I only make him worse.'

'It'll come,' said Mother. 'Don't keep worrying Sam about it. Once upon a time *you* couldn't whistle a tune either! Look at this plan – we've decided to keep *this* bit of garden. We can manage it quite well by ourselves. The rest will go with Green Meadows, but, of course, it will still seem like ours because Ellen Surrey says we may go there whenever we like.'

'And see all the animals,' said Sam. 'I'm going to visit all the old, old horses and donkeys each day. Mother, did you hear that Flash was going back to the shop?'

'Yes. Not yet, though,' said Mother. 'Sid's uncle is

well again, and some of the sheds are rebuilt, because he was insured, after all. He's buying a new little cart for Flash, and so our little pony will once more trot round the village with it!'

'He's had a lovely holiday,' said Clare. 'What's Sid going to do, Mother? Go back to his brother? We *shall* miss him!'

'No. He told me last night that his brother is managing well by himself, and so Sid isn't going back. You won't guess what job he's got!' said Mother.

'What?' asked the children.

'He's asked Ellen Surrey if she will take him on as gardener!' said Mother. 'He has got so fond of Green Meadows, and enjoyed doing the garden so much. He can't bear to give it up to another gardener!'

'Oh! Then we'll see Sid every day!' said Clare, delighted. 'I was afraid that if a strange gardener came he wouldn't like us running in and out of our old garden – but Sid won't mind a bit!'

The workmen came and began to work on the stables. Joe was with them, because Mother had asked the builder to give him a job. Joe was pleased. 'First you do me a good turn and let me keep my pigeons here,' he said. 'Then I do you a good turn back, and mend up things a bit for you. And now you've done me a good turn again! Well, it's my turn now to do something – and I'm going to work on these stables for you as well as I can!'

The job went very well indeed. The weather was good, and the men were good too. It was arranged that the family should go away for two months' holiday when school broke up in July, and that would allow the men to get on with the repairs to Green Meadows while it was empty. When the family came back, the stables would be ready for them to live in – a quaint little house with a pretty garden of its own, and pigeons flying about everywhere. There were twelve of them now, for they had laid eggs and hatched out babies that summer.

Each of the children owned one. Francis had one called Bobbo, Clare's was called Clapper because he clapped his wings so loudly, and Sam called his White-wings. They all came flying when they were called.

School broke up. Holidays came – and Granny went off with the children to a little house by the sea, leaving Mother and Mrs Oldham to strip Green Meadows of carpets and curtains, and to put the furniture into store till the stables were ready.

'Mother won't work too hard, will she?' said Francis, anxiously, to Granny, after they had said goodbye to her.

'No. Mrs Oldham will see to that,' said Granny. 'Now that I have sold Green Meadows and got the money, I can do lots of things I couldn't before. Go for this long holiday, for instance – and pay Mrs Oldham to come and help Mother every day.'

'I hope Rex and Dapple and the rest will be all right,' said Clare. 'I don't like leaving them. I'm glad Flash has gone happily back to his master. I saw him yesterday, trotting along pulling his new little vegetable cart – and oh, Granny, he saw me, and he came right over to me, cart and all!'

Mother joined them down by the sea in two weeks' time, and they all had a wonderful time. They were as brown as berries, even Mother. They tried to persuade Granny to swim, but she wouldn't. 'You can wear your chains too, if you think you'll miss their jingling,' said Sam, and got a tap on his hand!

They went back in September. Mother had gone ahead to see the furniture moved in, and curtains put up. Mrs Oldham was there to greet her, and Rex too.

Dan had proved a great standby. He had taken on the care of the pigeons, the rabbit, the guinea pig, Dapple, and Mr Black while the Green Meadows family had been away. Pongo the puppy had gone on a holiday with the family who owned him. It was a lovely thing for Dan to do, actually, because he had plenty of time to spare in the holidays and was up at Green Meadows all day long – while his mother cleaned up the rooms in the stables as they were finished.

The day came for the children and Granny to go back. They were in a great state of excitement – and when they saw the dear little house awaiting them, they were even more excited! It looked lovely, clean and gay and welcoming. And there was Mother on the doorstep, smiling all over her face!

'Let's explore, let's explore!' cried Clare, and they went all over the house at once, exclaiming in delight.

'There's a lot to be done yet,' said Mother. 'Sam's

bedroom isn't finished, nor are two of the rooms downstairs, and there's some more painting to be done. But at any rate it was ready enough to move into!'

'If only Daddy could see it!' said Clare. 'When's he coming home, Mummy! He's been away *too* long!'

'Sir Giles is coming to see me about him tomorrow,' said Mother. 'I'll tell you what he says.'

The surgeon came in next day with Duke, who had been staying with his old master. He fell upon Francis with joy. The boy hugged him. The dog was very dear to him because of that dreadful night in the early summer.

'I've come for two things,' said Sir Giles. 'One is to say that your husband will be home by Christmas, Mrs Marshall. At last we have got to the root of the matter and now I hope we can make headway.'

'Will he walk?' asked Mother, almost in a whisper.

'He'll hobble – I can't say more than that,' said Sir Giles. 'But he'll have no more pain, and he can certainly take some sort of job – brainwork, I mean. Wait and see; I'm quite hopeful now. And anyway he'll be home for Christmas.'

'What's the second thing you've come about?' said Mother.

'It's about Duke,' said Sir Giles. 'I have to go away again, this time to America. I don't want to leave him in Bill's care again. I want to give him to Francis – for his own dog. I know he loves him, and there's no doubt that Duke loves him back with all his heart. He's really more Francis's dog than mine. Will you have him, Francis?'

Would he have Duke! Francis couldn't believe his

ears. He went bright scarlet, and couldn't say a word.
But Duke said plenty!

'Woof! Woof-woof! Woof!' And he leapt on Francis
and licked him on all the bare places he could find!

'Oh,' said Francis, at last. 'Yes, I'll have him. I always
wanted a dog like Duke. Thank you very very much. Can
you really spare him?'

'Only to you,' said Sir Giles, with a smile. 'I'll come
and see him sometimes when I'm back again. May I leave
him here now, Mrs Marshall?'

So Duke came to live with them, and was the happiest
dog in the kingdom. For the first few days Francis went
about with his arm round Duke's neck, the dog trotting
beside him. He simply couldn't believe that Duke was
really his!

The days flew by. Christmas came nearer and nearer.
Daddy wrote cheerful letters, and said he was out of his
chair and hobbling with two sticks to visit other patients
in the ward. The next letter said he had hobbled too
much and was in bed again. The next one said he was up
once more. Would he be all right for Christmas?

'He's coming!' said Mother, one day, looking up from
a letter. 'He's coming next week – two days before
Christmas! Bill is to fetch him in Sir Giles's car, by Sir
Giles's own orders. How good he is!'

'What else does Daddy say?' asked Sam.

'He says he has a big surprise for us all,' said Mother.
'Bless him, I expect he's been working hard at making
some wonderful present for us. They have a fine
workshop at that hospital, you know, to help patients to

pass the time. Fancy – next week! And at the end of *this* week the workmen will be out and we'll have the house to ourselves.'

'That four-leaved clover was lucky after all,' said Francis. 'I began to think it was a fraud!'

Mother got ready for Christmas in the new little house. It hadn't a name yet, for nobody could think of a nice enough one. The Christmas tree arrived and stood in the hall, gaily decorated. The children put up paper chains and picked red-berried holly from the Green Meadows garden, with Sid's help. Mysterious parcels were hidden in every corner.

The day came for Daddy's arrival home. It was the first thought everyone had when they awoke that morning. 'Daddy's coming!'

What time would the car arrive? Nobody knew exactly. But at three o'clock, which was the earliest it *could* come, all the children were at the gate. Their front gate was now the one that used to be the back gate. It was mended, and painted white. Daddy had been told to come to that gate, though Bill himself knew that quite well, of course. Bill said he would help Daddy to hobble up to the house, and would even carry him, if necessary.

Three o'clock. Half-past three. Four o'clock. Oh dear! Would Daddy never come? Quarter-past four! Mother called from the door.

'Come up to the house for a minute, dears, and take a bun each, in case Daddy is very late. You had your dinner so early.'

They all ran up – but just as they were taking their

buns, they heard the sound of a car stopping outside.

'Daddy's come! Daddy's come!' squealed Clare, and dropped her bun to run to the gate.

Yes, there was the big car. As they got to the gate, the car door swung open, and a man leapt out. He walked briskly to the gate, smiling all over his face.

'Daddy!' screamed Clare. 'Daddy! You're walking!' She ran to him and he swung her up in his arms. Then Sam came running, wide-eyed and wondering, and last of all Francis. Sam looked at his father's legs. Yes, they were walking. And Daddy hadn't even got *one* stick! Sam threw his arms round his father's waist and buried his head in his coat. To have a father who *walked* – what a truly wonderful thing!

Mother heard the excitement and came running, bright-eyed and breathless. When she saw Daddy walking, with the three children clinging to him, she stopped, amazed.

'John! Oh, *John* !' she said and ran to him in joy. 'Was *this* your surprise? Oh, I never thought of that! Welcome home to us all – we've missed you so much!'

Granny jingled down the path with Mr Black behind, and met them halfway. Her eyes were full of happy tears. At last, at last, Daddy was well.

'Yes. I'm absolutely all right!' he said, smiling round. 'Stand away from me. See me jump! See me run! And on New Year's Eve Mother and I are going to a dance – do you hear that, Mother? No, don't say you haven't a frock. I'm going to buy you the most beautiful one in the world!'

Half-laughing, half-crying, the little family went into the house. What a homecoming! How different Daddy was! Sam had never seen him like this before, and he stared at him as if he was something out of another world.

They all sat down to an enormous tea at last. 'There's one thing you've left me to do, I see,' said Daddy. 'You haven't given this dear little house a name!'

'We couldn't think of one,' said Mother. 'Oh dear – to think of all that's happened this year, John. I was so miserable at the beginning. Do you remember, Francis, you and I went out into the garden in February. You made me come – and I told you all my troubles.'

'I remember,' said Francis. 'And you stooped and rang the bell of the very first snowdrop – oh, Mother, you did, and said it was lucky. And it was, it was!'

'Then,' said Daddy, at once, 'I here and now name this little house Snowdrop Cottage – and may it bring us as much good luck as the ringing of the first snowdrop bell this year!'

'Oh *yes* – Snowdrop Cottage – it's a lovely name!' said Clare. 'We'll get Joe to paint it on the gate as soon as ever he can. Snowdrop Cottage!'

Sam listened happily, his solemn face still turned towards this new and astonishing father. He pursed up his mouth and began to whistle. He whistled very loudly indeed, because he was so very happy.

Everybody turned and looked at him. 'Sam!' said Clare, in wonder. 'You're whistling a *tune!* A real *tune* !'

Sam stopped, delighted. 'What is it, then?' he asked. red in the face.

'The best one you *could* whistle!' said Clare. '"It's a Hap-Hap-Happy Day!"'